Inside Robin's Too Tight Tights

First Edition

Published by The Nazca Plains Corporation
Las Vegas, Nevada
2008

ISBN: 978-1-934625-91-0

Published by

The Nazca Plains Corporation ®
4640 Paradise Rd, Suite 141
Las Vegas NV 89109-8000

PUBLISHER'S NOTE
Inside Robin's Too Tight Tights is a work of fiction created wholly by *Tim Desmondes'*
imagination. All characters are fictional and any resemblance to any persons living
or deceased is purely by accident. No portion of this book reflects any real person
or events.

Cover, MAXFX
Art Director, Blake Stephens

Dedication

This book is dedicated to the rascals of this world (of whom I hope I am one.)

As my father said, "What's the use of being a fellow unless you're a Hell of a fellow?"

(Well, Dad. You were a bit of a rascal yourself. And relished the title. My hat's off to you.)

Inside Robin's Too Tight Tights

First Edition

Tim Desmondes

Contents

INTRODUCTION

The Robin Hood ballads, which are the source of the original tales about the English outlaw, were composed and sung by minstrels over a span of two centuries.

Despite the time span over which the lays and ballads were composed and the varied authorship of those lays and ballads, we feel we know Robin.

But much of what we believe we know comes from children's books and swashbuckling movies. From those bowdlerized versions of the lusty old ballads we learned that Robin robbed from the rich and gave to the poor. He led a band of some seven score Merrymen. He was an adept archer who poached on the king's deer in Sherwood and Barnsdale. He and his men were attired in Lincoln green. His nemesis was the proud Sheriff of Nottingham.

Robin's characteristics include bravado, insolence, loyalty, piety, and a sense of humor

He was pious but disdained churchmen. He was patriotic but disregarded his country's laws. He respected women and had a girlfriend called Maid Marian.

What the children's books and the movies leave out that the minstrels were clear about was that Robin was husky, hung, and horny.

One of the minstrels' pleasantries was that Robins' tights were often too tight.

I have attempted in the following rendering of the tale to give Robin's balls and his tight tights back to him. I'm sure he'll welcome their return.

For my more scholarly readers, I have included some ballad material in the language and dialect in which it has been transmitted to our times.

The minstrels placed our hero in various reigns depending on the

1

politics of the time of their performance. I have chosen to place Robin's lusty adventures in the reign of Henry II, Eleanor of Aquitaine, and Richard I.

TIM DESMONDES

Lythe and listin, gentilmen,
That be of freborne blode:
I shall you tel of a gode yeman[1]
His name was Robyn Hode.

Robyn was a prude outlaw,
Whyles he walked on grounde
So courteyse an outlawe as he was one
Was never non yfounde.

A Gest of Robyn Hode
The First Fytte
Circa 1300 A.D.

---

[1]   For readers interested in checking meanings of archaic words, see pages 177-180

CHAPTER ONE

The Teenage Outlaw

Robin was a lusty youth of eighteen years. He loved love, and, even more, he loved lust.

So lusty was he that he often wandered through his forested county sporting a valiant hardon.

Robin had a paramour named Rosalind who also loved love. And she felt a very warm attraction to his awesome erect manhood.

But she was virginally inclined and resisted all of Robin's heartfelt entreaties. Virgin she was. And virgin she intended to remain.

Rosalind would not be moved. She willingly allowed Robin's lips to kiss her passionately. She allowed his hands a great deal of freedom as they made free with her tits. She favored his cock with ministrations of her lovely hands and her pneumatic lips. But to perform the conjugal act she was adamantly opposed.

Yet, in every other way, Rosalind was not only available but eager to give and take in the game of love. So Robin took her one failing philosophically and was not one to mope about what apparently was resolutely resisted.

Early in the merry month of May, when Robin and Rosalind were happily enjoying themselves in the hayloft of her barn with kissing, groping, fondling, and sucking, the happy couple had idled away a few hours in their favorite pursuits and were resting contentedly in each other's arms.

"I heard that the Sheriff of Nottingham is sponsoring an archery match in Nottingham Town tomorrow," Robin mentioned to his love.

"Can you guess what the prize is for the winner of the sheriff's meet?" Robin continued, mischief in his eyes.

Rosalind could not guess.

"A butt of good October ale," Robin informed her.

Rosalind had a thirst for good, humming ale. And of all ales, October brew was by far her favorite.

"Oh, Robin," she exclaimed. "Go enter the shooting match. Win the contest and bring me back a butt of good October ale."

Robin sniffed an opportunity. He really was an excellent archer. He had never lost a contest, and when he went hunting he always hit his mark. He hoped he might be able to parlay the gift of the ale into the attainment of his libidinous desire. Namely hitting the mark between his sweetheart's thighs.

"Suppose I did go down to Nottingham Town," he said, thinking fast and craftily. "And suppose I won the butt and brought it back so you could wet your lips with your favorite brew. What might be my meed?"

"What do you mean?" the fair maid replied saucily. "You would get to show off how well you shoot, and you'd be pleasing me. *That* would be your meed."

"Tell me, Love," Robin further inquired, pressing the point. "What would you do to show your appreciation for the fairing of a butt of such humming ale?"

"For a butt of October Ale?" Rosalind replied. "Just about anything you want of me."

"You know what I've wanted of you for a long time," Robin prompted.

"Are you suggesting," the damsel rejoined, "that if you win the butt of ale and bring it to me, you would expect me to…?"

"To…play the two-backed beast," Robin proposed. "That is, to demonstrate how well I shoot into the target I have coveted since we met."

Rosalind thought it over. She really would like to have a nice butt of October ale. And she had been finding it more and more difficult to resist Robin's urgings anyway. At the moment the proposal appeared a possible fair exchange to her.

"Bring me the butt of ale," she told Robin, "and I will consider your offer seriously."

Robin felt so confident of his archery ability that he anticipated he would finally, the next evening, at last, insert his love arrow into the choicest target he could imagine.

He was a happy young man indeed.

The next morning, bow in hand, and loaded quiver over shoulder, Robin set out from Locksley Hall for Nottingham Town through Sherwood Forest. As usual, he whistled his merry tune and sported his pleasant hardon. He felt quite satisfied with himself. He had never been bested in an archery match and saw no reason why he should not be returning to Locksley with a butt of ale and the possibility of the long-awaited, hoped-for fuck.

Along the way, Robin chanced upon a clearing. In that glade he observed fifteen foresters and ten young ladies. Five of the foresters were fully clothed in Lincoln green. But the other ten were naked as the beasts of the forest. And the ten maids?...There was not a stitch covering their fair bodies. In the midst of the cavorting party was a large keg of ale. And it was clear to the young archer that the entire group had drawn generously from the keg. For everyone appeared very merry indeed. The couples were clearly engaged in the act Robin sought to claim from Rosalind.

One of the foresters who was more rotund than the others was fully clothed and ogling the lusty pranks of the naked villagers. As this corpulent forester glanced away from the frolickers to lift a horn of ale to his lips, he spied Robin strolling down the path. Young Robin of Locksley Hall was known in the neighborhood, and the forester recognized him.

The forester was just drunk enough to think it would be great fun to bait the lad.

"What ho!" he shouted at Robin. "What is a youngster like you doing lumbering along here with your youthful hardon. And why are you hauling a big bow like that? And to what purpose do you tote all those arrows in your quiver?"

Robin did not take affronts from anyone.

Just to show the churlish forester that he could handle bow and arrow with deftness, Robin drew an arrow from his quiver, nocked it to his bowstring and surveyed the area. There was a herd of deer grazing at the far reaches of the glade with a noble buck standing at the fore.

"See that hart?" the lad challenged the forester. "Let us say he is the target. Now, watch my arrow."

With that, Robin let fly the arrow which, in turn, felled the hart clean.

"Let that be a warning to you, Knave," the youthful archer advised. "Do not make light of Robin Hood."

"No one insults me, Master Hood," the drunken forester slurred. "I'll take care of you right here in the forest and no one will ever be the wiser. Drop your cock and say your prayers."

The forester stooped down to the ground to pick up his yew bow and a clothyard arrow. There was no question that he meant to shoot Robin. And none of his drunken group demonstrated any intention of stopping him.

Robin was a hot-blooded lad and reacted to the threat instinctively. Before the forester could nock an arrow onto his bowstring, Robin, with lightning speed, had his own arrow tightly strung and aimed. With speed born of self-preservation Robin unloosed his arrow. And the arrow found its home in the rude forester's heart. The varlet fell to the glade's leafy floor quite dead.

The attending party sobered up immediately. Everything had occurred very quickly and the former merrymakers were struck dumb. They stared at their fallen companion then at the young man who had killed him. No one seemed to know what to do.

Robin was aware that he was outnumbered. But it was also quite clear to him that the people staring from him to his victim were not in any condition to pursue if he moved right away.

Twenty nude frolickers chasing a lone youth through the forest seemed an unlikely scene. The revelers would have to clothe themselves prior to pursuit.

So he headed off the path and entered the forest wilderness. He circled around and headed back for Locksley Hall.

It would have been folly to continue on to Nottingham town under the circumstances.

Meanwhile the four clothed foresters somberly dragged their defunct friend to Nottingham town and to the sheriff's office. The members of the remaining group, all nude, realized there was nothing productive they could do about the situation. So they shrugged their shoulders, dipped their drinking horns back into the ale keg and returned to their drunken fucking.

As Robin wended his way homeward he was aware that his life had been radically changed by the two rash acts he had committed. He had killed a man. That carried a capital punishment. But, worse yet, he had poached one of the king's deer. That put a price on his head of two hundred pounds. Which meant bounty hunters would be out searching for him to drag him to justice. Two hundred pounds was a pretty sum. Robin knew he would have to avoid and evade bounty hunters for the rest of his life.

Robin was now an outlaw and would henceforth have to seek refuge there within the forests of Sherwood and Barnsdale.

Robin sped back to Locksley Hall and found his faithful servant Pym. He explained to Pym what had happened. He gave his servant the choice to either remain on the estate and watch over matters there or follow his master into a life outside the law. Pym did not have to consider twice. He was loyal to his master and swore to follow him wherever the trail might lead.

Robin and Pym rounded up tools and clothing to take into the forest as a foundation for the outdoor life. They gathered a hatchet, an ax, a spade, a set of knives, and other necessities for living in the greenwood.

What they could not find readily available were jerkins and tights.

They had everything else in readiness to depart for the greenwood. But Robin had another matter to attend to first. He followed the lane to the manse where his Rosalind lived. He whistled thrice outside her window. That was the signal he always used to let her know he would await her in the stables.

In minutes the lovers met in the loft of the stable, tumbling onto the fragrant hay.

While Pym waited patiently at a discreet distance from the stables guarding the bundles that he and Robin would carry into the safety of the greenwood, the lad and Rosalind had need to say goodbye in lusty style.

Robin explained to Rosalind what had happened to him in the forest glade.

"So, Dear, I have to leave you and go live an outlaw's life in the greenwood. Will you miss me?"

"I will miss you, Robin. I will miss you grievously."

"Then might you be about to grant me a special gift to remember you by?" the lad asked.

"You mean…?" she asked, knowing very well what he meant.

"I would really like for us to make love, uniting us in the way of man and woman," quoth Robin.

"I don't see that butt of October ale anywhere," his paramour japed.

"You know I never got to Nottingham Town and the contest," Robin rebutted, still hoping his sweetling was just joshing about still expecting the damnèd ale.

"No ale, no fuck," Rosalind replied firmly.

Robin realized this was no time to quibble. Let Rosalind remain virginal if that was what she insisted on.

With stoic resignation, Robin let her suck him off and bade her a fond adieu.

Frustrated but not desolated by getting only a blow job, the young master of Locksley Hall rejoined Pym and the two of them faded into the depths of the greenwood.

Meanwhile the four foresters hauled the corpse of their fallen companion to the home of the Sheriff of Nottingham. When they aroused the sheriff, they told him that their friend and companion had been foully murdered while he was dutifully guarding the king's deer in the forest.

"Who has done this foul deed?" asked the sheriff.

"Master Robin Hood of Locksley Hall," was the reply.

The sheriff knew of the lad, of course, although he did not know him by sight.

"But why did the young man draw on your co-worker?" the sheriff inquired.

"Because Geoffrey caught the miscreant poaching on the king's herd. Master Robin shot a magnificent hart."

The sheriff was *very* interested in that bit of information.

So, this young man had shot a deer. The sheriff could do very nicely, himself, with a two hundred pound bounty from good King Harry. He silently vowed that he would personally bring the malefactor to the king's justice and see him hanged publicly where three roads meet as warning to all who would so much as consider poaching in the Forest of Sherwood.

Whilst the sheriff pondered lucrative thoughts, Robin and Pym discovered a sequestered spot near the Great Oak that centers Sherwood Forest.[2] They constructed a hut between the oak and Clough Creek.

Robin proved to be an excellent woodsman. With his yew bow and goose-quilled arrows he provided the two of them with meat aplenty from King Henry's deer. Pym gathered fruits and berries. He butchered the meat and roasted it over a firepit he built. Robin and Pym were quite self-sufficient.

However, they needed an animal to carry provisions for them. Robin made a visit to Kelham where he knew Lord Kelham kept a herd of asses. Milord never visited his lands in Nottinghamshire, preferring the pleasures of London Town to bucolic pursuits. So Robin liberated a sturdy ass from the herd, named her Gertrude, and rode her back to his forest retreat.

While Robin roamed the forest in search of meat and adventure, Pym kept the hut clean, performed the necessary chores, prepared the meals, and went to market in Bleasby astride Gertrude. Pym was unknown in Bleasby and was never molested by inquisitive villagers. From Bleasby's markets he brought to Robin's forest home oats, flour, salt, and kegs of ale.

He spotted the shop of the local clothier. Knowing full well that he and his master had departed Locksley Hall without the jerkins and tights necessary for life in the forest, he ordered two jerkins and two pairs of tights.

"I would like one pair small size and the other large."

"I am sorry," replied the clothier. "In Bleasby, all we carry is one size. It fits all."

So Pym bought the one-size-fits-all size. And he knew Robin would prefer the ensemble in Lincoln green.

With their shelter, their skills and their provisions, Robin and Pym lived in the greenwood like kings.

Yes, Robin was pleased with the purchases.

But when he and Pym tried out the clothing, it turned out that one-size-fits-all fit Pym a bit loosely. And that size fit Robin snugly. Not just somewhat snuggly. *Very* tight.

The tights fit *so* tight that the outline of his cock and balls caused those appendiges to show through quite prominently.

He decided he would just have to accommodate to the discomfort.

But since he was of priapic bent, it was not long before he sprang a hardon.

"Oh, my God!" our hero bellowed. "The pain is excruciating."

And, being a very brave fellow who seldom complained, you just know it hurt like Hell.

He reached his right hand down into the tights, twisted the anguished

---

2   The *trystell-tre* of the ballads.

member sideways to the right, and led it into a comfortable upright position.

He vowed to wear his dong in an upright position every time it was ensconced in his tights.

Anything to avoid that penile discomfort.

It was Maytime in Sherwood Forest. And in that merry month, the lassies who lived on the skirts of the Forest and in the nearby towns and hamlets came a-Maying into the greenwood. They collected posies for their nosegays, garlands and chaplets. They wore the flowers in their hair and around their necks, and gathered them into bouquets in their hands.

Three damsels had come together to gather flowers and to find adventure in the forest. They had gathered as many posies as they could carry and went in search of further adventure.

At the time the lassies were plucking flowers, Robin was enjoying his mid-day repast. Pym had prepared a collation of salt venison pie and sun-dried apples. The meal engendered a great thirst in Robin, which he quenched with an overabundance of ale. The combination of the warm May afternoon, a bellyful of hearty food, and a bladderful of cool humming ale caused a pleasant somnolence to overcome the young fugitive.

He lay down under the soft shade of the greenwood and slipped into a dreamless slumber.

The three maids who were about to return home from their Maying happened upon the napping youth. None could suppress her giggles.

Robin awoke to the pleasant sound of female laughter.

He drowsily extended his arms in loving greeting. But the lethargy of his condition held him fast to the forest floor.

The lassies consulted each other how to have sport with the helpless handsome youth.

Bess, the sauciest of the three, held a nosegay of forest flowers above the lad's face, causing him to sneeze. Despite his sneezing fit, Robin laughed heartily with the maids.

Dorothy, a brown-haired beauty, kissed Robin once on each cheek.

Robin begged her for a kiss on the mouth, but was rewarded with only a sweet smile for his trouble.

The third of the damsels had her own proclivities.

She spied the massive bulge at the crotch of Robin's tights, breathed warm breath on the spot, and ran her dainty hand up and down the length of the member.

Unfortunately for Robin, he had neglected to secure that member in an upright position after he had last relieved himself.

"Ow!...God damn!" he cried out as his right hand swept inside his tights.

By the time he had righted the situation, all thoughts of Rosalind flew out of his mind.

Once the three merry nymphs had fully satisfied themselves with teasing their willing victim, they arose with one accord and fled away from the glade.

With youthful agility Robin regained his footing but was still somewhat groggy despite the painful awakening he had experienced.

"O, Ladies. Do not run away without even giving me your names," he shouted.

"Yours first," Dorothy cried back, over her shoulder.

"Robin Hood of Locksley Hall, at your service any time," he shouted.

"They call me Bess," the sauciest one called back.

"And I am Dorothy," claimed the brown-haired beauty.

The three maids were disappearing into the surrounding copse when Robin desperately called out, "And you, Lass of the Flaxen Hair. What is your name?"

The damsel who had aroused his slumbering cock with a soft breath and a grazing hand called back, "I am called Maid Marian. Search me out if you can. I find you a youth to my taste."

And she disappeared from view.

Robin cried for joy. As already mentioned, forgotten was his Rosalind. He was infused with a new love. She who would forever be his one true love was named Maid Marian. Robin treasured her name in his heart.

In his first months of wandering Sherwood Forest, Robin came upon a hundred other fugitive yeomen hiding in the greenwood. These were men who were suffering from unjust accusations or from unlawful seizure of their lands. Robin gathered nearly seven score of them into a jolly band, named them his Merrymen, and was chosen by them to be their unquestioned leader.

In the sequestered heart of the forest, near the Giant Oak and Clough Creek, the Merrymen built huts of bark and branches. They constructed cots of sweet rushes and the skins of forest beasts. The fellowship erected a feasting area on the sward consisting of benches, tables, firepits, and tuns. Guards were always on post to see that the outside world could not intrude on their domain.

Among the needed supplies were garments – jerkins and tights of Lincoln green.

There were varied reactions among the men when they donned their merry garb. Those who were lightly endowed in the genital area had no problems. Those with medium sized equipment had some adjustments to make when they got horny. But those with robust pizzles found that one-size-fits-all tights offer a challenge when aroused.

Robin demonstrated how to minimize the bane.

Pym was appointed master of the outdoor kitchen and each man served under him in rotation to roast, stir, and broil the victuals that filled their lusty bellies.

Each and every man of them had been unjustly despoiled by baron, knight, squire, bishop or abbot. Robin required of each of those who chose to join his band a vow that he would despoil those oppressors, seize what had been squeezed from the poor, and re-distribute that wealth to the downtrodden.

With the lucre Robin and his Merrymen exacted from the rich, Robin sent Pym to Barnsdale or Bleasby for purchases. Everything not expended on maintaining the lifestyle of the hardy band was distributed to the poor.

When word was spread to the trampled and oppressed who were barely able to hold body and soul together, those grateful poor came into the confines of Sherwood Forest and there received the wherewithal to survive and even thrive. There was never an instance of any beneficiary of the largess of the Merrymen betraying the outlaw band.

They happened to meet on a long narrow bridge,
And neither of them would give way;
Quoth bold Robin Hood, and sturdily stood,
"I'll show you right Nottingham way."

With that from his quiver an arrow he drew,
A broad arrow with a goose-wing.
The stranger reply'd, "I'll liquor thy hide,
If thou offerst to touch the string."

Quoth bold Robin Hood, "Thou doest prate like an ass,
For were I to bend but my bow,
I could send a dart quite thro thy proud heart,
Before thou couldst strike me one blow."

"Thou talkst like a coward," the stranger reply'd;
"Well armd with a long bow, you stand,
To shoot at my breast, while I, I protest
Have nought but a staff in my hand."

"The name of a coward," quoth Robin, "I scorn,
Wherefore my long bow I'll lay by.
And now, for thy sake, a staff I will take,
The truth of thy manhood to try."

Then Robin Hood stept to a thicket of trees,
And chose him a staff of ground-oak.
Now this being done, away he did run
To the stranger, and merrily spoke:

"Lo! see my staff, it is lusty and tough,
Now here on the bridge we will play.
Whoever falls in, the other shall win
The battle, and so we'll away."

"With all my whole heart," the stranger reply'd,
"I scorn in the least to give out."
This said, they fell to't without more dispute,
And their staffs they did flourish about.

And first Robin he gave the stranger a bang,
So hard that it made his bones ring.
The stranger he said, "This must be repaid,
I'll give you as good as you bring.

So long as I'm able to handle my staff,
To die in your debt, friend, I scorn."
Then to it each goes, and followd their blows,
As if they had been threshing of corn.

The stanger gave Robin a crack on the crown,
Which caused the blood to appear.
Then Robin, enrag'd, more fiercely engag'd,
And followed his blows more severe.

So thick and fast did he lay it on him,
With a passionate fury and ire,
At every stroke, he made him to smoke,
As if he had been all on fire.

O then into fury the stranger he grew,
And gave him a damnable look.
And with it a blow that laid him full low,
And tumbld him into the brook.

"I prithee, good fellow, O where art thou now?"
The stranger, in laughter, he cry'd.
Quoth bold Robin Hood, 'Good faith, in the flood,

And floating along with the tide.

"I needs must acknowledge thou art a brave soul.
With thee I'll no longer contend.
For needs must I say, thou hast got the day,
Our battle shall be at an end."

Then unto the bank he did presently wade,
And pulld himself out by a thorn.
Well done, at the last, he blowd a loud blast
Straitway on his fine bugle-horn.

The echo of which through the vallies did fly,
At which his stout bowmen appeard,
All clothd in green, most gay to be seen.
So up to their master they steerd.

"O what's the matter?" quoth William Stutely.
"Good master, you are wet to the skin."
"No matter,'" quoth he. "The lad which you see,
In fighting hath tumbld me in."

"He shall not go scot-free," the others reply'd.
So strait they were seizing him there,
To duck him likewise. But Robin Hood cries,
"He is a stout fellow, forbear.

"There's no one shall wrong thee, friend, be not afraid.
These bowmen upon me do wait.
There's threescore and nine. If thou wilt be mine,
Thou shalt have my livery strait.

And other accoutrements fit for a man.
Speak up, jolly blade, never fear.
I'll teach you also the use of the bow,
To shoot at the fat fallow deer."

"O here is my hand," the stranger reply'd.
"I'll serve you with all my whole heart.
My name is John Little, a man of good mettle.
Nere doubt me, for I'll play my part."

"His name shall be alterd," quoth William Stutely.
"And I will his godfather be.
Prepare then a feast, and none of the least,
For we will be merry," quoth he.

They presently fetchd in a brace of fat does,
With humming strong liquor likewise.
They loved what was good, so in the green wood,
This pretty sweet babe they baptize.

He was, I must tell you, but seven foot high,
And, may be an ell in the waist.
A pretty sweet lad. Much feasting they had,
Bold Robin the christening grac'd.

With all his bowmen, which stood in a ring,
And were of the Nottingham breed,
Brave Stutely comes then, with seven yeomen,
And did in this manner proceed.

"This infant was called John Little," quoth he.
"Which name shall be changed anon.
The words we'll transpose, so where-ever he goes,
His name shall be calld Little John."

They all with a shout made the elements ring
So soon as the office was o're.
To feasting they went, with true merriment,
And tippld strong liquor galore.
Francis James Child, *The English and Scottish Popular Ballads,* Volume III, Number 125.
1888

CHAPTER TWO

Robin and LittleJohn

One merry morn in June, with the forest in full bloom, Robin and his Merrymen arose and, as always, plunged heads and hands into the bubbling waters of Clough Creek. They assembled on the sward and broke their fast with venison, oatcakes and honey, accompanied by humming ale.

After breakfast, Robin was itching for adventure and strode out alone, yew bow and oaken cudgel in hand and arrow-filled quiver and horn slung over his broad shoulders. Before he left camp he bade his Merrymen tarry in the greenwood, but harken well for his horn. If sore need befell him, he would blast thrice on his horn and beckon them to his aid.

He followed Clough Creek, accompanied only by his own whistling and hardon, in a north-easterly direction towards Tuxford Town. This led him on a shaded path through bird-haunted dell and around forest skirts.

The trail veered northwest, leading Robin back to Clough Creek. At this point in the forest trail there was a narrow wooden bridge spanning the waters. Robin took a sighting beyond the bridge and spied a burly giant of a man approaching from the other side.

Robin sped his gait in order to cross the bridge first. And as he did so, the stranger quickened his step as well.

"Halt, Stranger," Robin called out. "I, the better man, shall cross yon bridge first. You may wait your turn there on the other side until I have finished my crossing."

The stranger called back in a strong, sure voice.

"You are right, callow youth. The better man will, indeed, cross the bridge first. Which means it will be me and not some mere snot-nosed youngster."

"Is that so!" responded Robin, quickening his step still more. "We will see about that."

The stranger did not appear to be carrying any weaponry save a blackthorn staff, which was very much in evidence.

The stranger and Robin appeared at the foot of the bridge simultaneously, the large man on one side, and Robin on the other.

"You step on this bridge at your peril," the stranger announced, swinging his staff above his head until it whistled.

"I am armed with bow and arrow," Robin replied. "I am not a craven and will set down that weaponry, if you allow me to do so. I would rather fight you man to man than shoot an arrow at a man armed only with a staff."

"I will wait," responded the burly stranger. "I see you have an oaken cudgel. If you are man enough to fight me fair, staff to staff, we shall see who rules this bridge."

Robin laid his bow and quiver on the path.

Each man stepped upon the bridge at the same time. Each was armed with only a stick, the one with his blackthorn staff and the other with his oaken cudgel. And each whistled a happy tune to show his disdain for the skill of the opponent.

The stranger towered above Robin by a head and a neck. His shoulders exceeded Robin's by the breadth of two palms. And his waist measured at least an ell. But Robin believed his own youth, audacity, sprightliness and daring were a match for the size and weight of his burly opponent.

The contestants marched directly towards each other and met in the middle of the bridge.

The stranger whirled his blackthorn staff in the air until it whistled a tune of its own. Robin was not intimidated by its song.

"One of us, and one of us alone, shall stand upon this bridge," claimed Robin. "Prepare to bathe your butt in the creek as I knock your corpulence into those babbling waters."

"One of us will indeed bathe his arse in those waters," answered the stranger. "Let us hope the waters cleanse the snot from off your baby face."

With that, the fighters set to. Robin proved to be the more dexterous and supple. The stranger possessed greater strength and reach.

The clash of staff to cudgel was, indeed, very nearly evenly matched. At times the youth's spryness seemed to make Robin king of the bridge. Then the brawn of the stranger appeared to dominate. Neither man would yield willingly to the other. Each was determined to stand firm on the wooden bridge until one or the other was knocked into the singing waters that roiled beneath them.

The sound of the battle resounded through the forest. First, it drove the timid beasts away from the combat area. The Merrymen were aware of the tension in the forest, and followed in the direction from which the fauna was fleeing. Before long, there was a silent audience to the battle between the giant and the youth. None of the watchers would leave the shelter of the undergrowth to show his face to the battlers. A goodly number of the men in green would have loved to cheer their leader on. But all knew that Robin would not have anyone interfering with the joust, even by shouted support.

Bit by bit, Robin's stamina eroded. The stranger was relentless in his intensity. Robin began to realize that his arm and hand were losing the strength to continue swinging the oaken cudgel. With each swing the weapon seemed to become heavier and heavier. The stranger's strength and determination appeared to increase rather than diminish as time wore on.

Sweat was pouring down Robin's body. His lungs burned and gasped for air. His shoulder muscles ached excruciatingly. But he soldiered on. He was determined to win this match. In feats of daring, skill, and strength he had always prevailed. He had never known the meaning of defeat.

With every resource of his mind, body, and spirit Robin overcame his extreme fatigue and struck against the stranger. The stranger parried with his staff. Robin had to gasp for air. As he took that gasp his opponent whacked him so fairly clean that Robin lost his footing and tumbled off the bridge into the familiar waters of Clough Creek.

Robin was stunned as his body hit the water. He looked up and saw the stranger standing upright on the bridge, laughing uproariously.

Robin realized his ridiculous position, bobbing in the water, sopping wet. He burst out in raucous laughter at his own comic plight. The giant's whole frame shook with mirth. Robin matched him guffaw for guffaw.

The Merrymen continued to keep hidden in the underbrush. They did not have any idea how to respond to their leader's defeat. Holding one's peace seemed the best course of action at the moment.

Robin's horn was still hanging from the belt that was over his shoulder. He emptied the water out of it, put the horn to his lips and blasted thrice. The Merrymen scrambled out of the bushes onto the creek's shore. None knew what to do next so they awaited Robin's order.

Robin crawled out of the creek, dripping water like a fountain and laughing with mirth still.

"Lads," he said. "I want you to meet the finest opponent I have ever encountered. Three cheers for the stranger."

The cheers went up as the laughing stranger walked the remainder of the way across the bridge, extended his hand to Robin and the two men exchanged clasps of friendship.

Robin and the stranger could not stop laughing and fell to the ground until their sides ached from merriment.

When they had laughed themselves out, the two arose. They were surrounded by the green-garbed band.

"What a brave, stout fellow you are, Stranger," Robin said. "You deal with your staff with a skill I have never before seen.

"I would like to welcome you to join our merry band."

"What would that mean?" asked the large man.

"Join us and you will receive three suits of Lincoln green each year, plus forty marks in fee. You will feed on venison and quaff stout ale enough to keep that ample belly of yours satisfied. And you will share in whatever fortune we reap in our wooded domain. A finer group of hearty lads you will never find to associate with than these you see clustered about us. What say you, Fellow? Will you join us?"

"I don't know," the stranger answered carefully. "I know you as a man who handles a cudgel less well than I manipulate my blackthorn staff. That I can understand, for you stood against me far sturdier than any man I have met in the five surrounding shires. But I cannot join any man who cannot shoot an apple shaft less well than I. If you are a worthy archer I just might consider joining your green-clad throng."

"Fair enough," Robin answered. "That is a condition I can understand and respect. Will, cut a slice of bark from yonder tree and affix it to the oak tree that stands some fourscore yards distant."

Whilst Will Stutely set up the target as Robin had asked, the stranger examined the bows and arrows the Merrymen had brought with them. He chose the stoutest bow among them all. He then found an arrow that suited him. It was a gray goose shaft, well-feathered and straight.

The target was by then in view and Will had set a mark upon the ground.

The stranger toed the mark with his chosen bow and arrow in readiness. He nocked the arrow and drew the bowstring to his cheek. He aimed well and deftly loosed the arrow on the target. The arrow cloved the exact center of the bark.

The yeomen cheered at so fair a shot.

Robin took his trusty yew bow in hand and chose an arrow from his quiver. He knew that if he matched the stranger's shot he would add a worthy fellow to his band.

Robin stepped to the mark, aimed well, and let fly the feathered shaft toward the distant target. That arrow flew so straight and true that it hit the stranger's shaft squarely, splintering it to shreds.

The yeomen cheered their leader. But no one cheered more heartily than the stranger.

"I have never before beheld so true an archer," said the stranger. "I would be honored to join your band."

Robin clasped him on the shoulder.

"You are welcome, then. What is your name?"

"In my own country," answered the stranger, "I am known as John

Little."

"Here in the greenwood I will rechristen you," Robin replied. "For as long as you are a member of our jolly band you will be known as Littlejohn."

Littlejohn nodded his head in agreement. The Merrymen all cheered. Robin, Littlejohn, and the greenclad band proceeded to their dwellingplace beneath the Great Oak. Littlejohn's entry into the band increased its size to sevenscore men.

The company assembled to feast, drink, and make merry. They had assembled a brace of fat does and had them roasting well over great fires. They broached a keg of jolly good ale and old. The feast awaited the party.

Robin and his men sat on the benches on the green moss clearing. Robin took his place in the center and seated Littlejohn to his right.

"Brave band of brothers," he addressed the assemblage. "This day I have met a man whose strength and character I esteem greatly. I present to you, as second in command of our merry company, Littlejohn."

A giant cheer greeted Robin's statement. Then all fell to feasting and drinking rowdily.

When the feasting and quaffing was done and the belching had quieted, Will Stutely slipped quietly behind the bench where Littlejohn sat. Littlejohn was unaware that anyone was behind him.

Will had in hand a full horn of humming ale.

"Brothers," Will shouted. "I call upon you all to witness the rechristening of our newly acquired member and our revered second in command."

Will forthwith poured the full horn of ale over Littlejohn's head.

"I christen thee Littlejohn," Will proclaimed.

Littlejohn bore the jest in good spirit and joined his raucous laughter to that of the entire group.

Pym stepped forward and handed three jerkins and three pairs of tights to Robin.

Robin bade Littlejohn arise.

"Littlejohn," he said. "Welcome to our merry band. I promised that if you joined us, you would receive three suits of Lincoln green each year. In addition, enough food and ale to keep you robust. And, of course, a fair share in our fortune."

He extended the jerkins and tights.

"Now that you are baptized into our fellowship, here are the promised uniforms."

Littlejohn held up a pair of the tights and guffawed loudly enough to ring the welkin.

"I concur on all else, Chief," he roared. "But one part of your offer I cannot accept."

"And what is that?" wondered Robin.

Littlejohn stripped to complete nudity before his new companions.

Everyone before had been amazed at his enormous stature. But the jaws of over half of them gaped at the pecker that confronted them. It was more ample in size than could even be expected from such a stalwart frame.

The giant then attempted to get his feet into the one-size-fits-all garment.

It was rent into shreds.

Robin laughed heartily.

'Littlejohn," he gasped. "You shall remain a full-fledged member of our band.

"But, unlike the rest of us, you shall not be garbed in Lincoln green. Pym will go to town and purchase three ample garments of any color.

"None of us wants to have you try on another pair of tights. I don't believe any of us is up to feeling, again, the inferiority of our own pricks if ever confronted again with that awesome dong."

And thus Littlejohn became an accepted member of the Merrymen.

CHAPTER THREE

The Sign of the Blue Boar

The dusty highway that led from Nottingham to Lincoln skirted Sherwood Forest. Travelers on that road were accustomed to stop, rest, eat, and slake their thirst at the Sign of the Blue Boar.

It was an inviting tavern. Lovely trees stood all about it and the alehouse itself was covered with trailing clematis and sweet woodbine. Under a spreading oak that shaded the greensward in front of the tavern's door there were tables and chairs for travelers who enjoyed taking a pot of ale in the great outdoors. The beer was good at the Blue Boar. But the humming ale was more renowned. Mine host, Master Eadom, was of cheerful mien and of welcoming disposition. Mine hostess, Mistress Hyacinth, kept the hostelry orderly and was known to prepare the best shepherd pie in all Nottinghamshire.

Mine host kept a dog named Brian. Brian was of gentle disposition most of the time and wandered freely among the guests. But if Master Eadom set the beast upon any visitor who was intent on mischief, or on disrupting the peace of the inn, or who was recalcitrant about paying for his drink or fare, Brian turned surly. When Brian bared his teeth even the most unruly varlet readily behaved as he ought.

The serving wench, Maken, was comely, cheerful, and friendly. Although she plied a second trade at the Blue Boar, no one could call her bawd. For she disported herself only with those she chose, and in her own prescribed manner. And she chose only those customers who pleased her well

The pothouse was well known and often visited by Robin, Littlejohn, Will Stutely, David of Doncaster…in short by every last man of Robin's band. The Merrymen were known and recognized by Master Eadom, Mistress Hyacinth, Maken, and, of course, Brian. None of these would ever betray Robin or his men. For the Merrymen were among mine host's best customers. They never caused unpleasantness, and always paid their scores tidily.

One June day, after quaffing a morning pint at the Blue Boar, Robin was out and about in his search for Maid Marian. He could not rest until he found the beauteous lassie who had breathed gently on his cock and caressed it with her hand. She had claimed she found him to her taste.

He treasured her name in his heart and within his tights.

Maken, the serving wench, wished him good cess in his quest.

Robin was deeply in love with the flaxen- haired damsel. He had no clue about where she dwelt. But to find his true love again was Robin's great quest.

The lovestruck lad donned many a disguise as he visited every town, village, and hamlet that skirted the forest in search of his own, true love. He was a month into that quest.

On this particular morning, in the guise of an itinerant cutlery salesman and knife sharpener Robin set out from the Blue Boar to visit Worksop. He was whistling a merry tune as he entered the town. Up and down Worksop's byways he trudged with a bagful of wares, his whetting wheel, and his ever present oaken cudgel.

He called out, "Knives, shears, and cleavers. Knives, shears, and cleavers. Buy them, sharpen them. Good prices today."

The price Robin charged for his merchandise or for sharpening on his whetting stone depended on his customer's purse. A poor goodwife in rags and tatters paid a penny for what the squire's wife paid a pound or an angel. No one ever took Robin for anything ought but an itinerant salesman and sharpener. Certainly no one even considered that he might be Robin Hood, the notorious outlaw of Barnsdale and Sherwood Forest.

On a back street of Worksop the youthful outlaw glimpsed a lassie he recognized. Not a month previous she had teased him into a sneeze beneath the Great Oak of Sherwood Forest. He well remembered the name of the mischievous maid.

"Good morrow, Miss," he said when she was within hailing distance. "Knives, shears, or cleavers?"

"I have no need of such," replied the lass, right saucily.

"Can I sharpen up anything dull in your life?" the apparent knife sharpener asked in an insinuating tone.

The lass took a fresh look at the huckster. There was something about him that stirred a memory. What was it? Something associated with flowers and the greenwood.

"Do you not recognize me without a nosegay in my face, Bess," the young man asked in a voice that she recalled from an encounter in Sherwood

Forest. And the man knew her name. The puzzle was solving itself.

"You know my name," Bess said. "Where and when have we met?"

"We met beneath the Great Oak, Bess Darling. And at that place you sprinkled me with pollen."

Bess took a deep look at the green tights the knife sharpener wore. She well recognized the bulge at the crotch now.

Bess was now able to penetrate the disguise.

"Lord of mercy," she exclaimed. "Beneath that hat I recognize those lively eyes. Beneath that coat I will wager I would find a body garbed in Lincoln green. And within those tights I spy a manhood tightly held and facing North. You are Robin Hood of Sherwood Forest, are you not?"

Robin admitted it was indeed he. He asked her if she would like to regale him again with a posy.

Bess led Robin to her nearby cottage.

Once within the confines of her home, Bess ignored the bouquet in its vase, but directly bade Robin remove his knife sharpener's coat and caused him to stand at attention before her. She slipped his tights off his hips so that they slithered down to around his ankles. She removed her blouse so that her perky tits pointed provocatively at the bandit.

She invited him to caress her breasts, but forbade him to suck the cherry-red nipples.

She then proceeded to massage his cock with her dainty white hands.

Very skillful were those hands. She brought the turgid cock to the point where she observed pre-come at the tip. The sight, accompanied by the amatory fondling Robin was engaging in on her breasts, caused a warm dampening of her twat.

She ceased the soft up and down caresses she had been applying to his dong, and cradled his nuts in her delicate hand. She was not ready for the outlaw to come yet.

She needed to give attention to her hardened clitoris.

Robin was held breathless, in near agony, to be released of his wad.

But he waited patiently, massaging those deep-red nipples while Bess pleasured herself with her left hand whilst cradling his scrotum.

When she was about to spasm, she re-applied her right hand to his shaft. And with perfect precision slipped her fist up and down over his tool so that his orgasm matched her own.

The lad and lass laughed companionably at their simultaneous orgasm.

Having come, they were ready to re-clothe themselves.

Now clad they sat at Bess' table where they sipped a pot of October ale that Bess had fetched from the larder.

"And now, fair hustler," Bess said. "I know what it is you want. Information about where to find Maid Marian."

"Right you are," Robin agreed. "Is she still awaiting me?"

"Marian says you remain very much to her taste," Bess said with a merry laugh. "She admits to being in love with her Robin."

"And I remain in love with her," quoth Robin. "I have sought her every day since we parted. Tell me, then, Sweet Bess. Where can I find my heart's desire?"

"She will be available to you only if you prove industrious and true enough to find her," the saucy lassie advised him.

"Yes, yes," Robin said, expressing his excitement. "Therefore tell me where I may successfully search for my beloved."

"Maid Marian permitted me to grant you one clue. And one clue alone," Bess advised him. "She said to tell you she dwells at the end of the lane."

"The end of the lane?" Robin questioned. "That is hardly a fair clue. There is many a lane in Good King Harry's domain. Each has two ends. Tell me, Bess. At the end of which of King Henry and Queen Eleanor's roads does the flower of my heart dwell?"

"That I am sworn not to tell you," said Bess. "Maid Marian says that if you truly love her, you will discover the lane."

Robin left the house, his disguise in his bag and his cudgel in his hand.

No one recognized the youth as he trudged the road from Worksop to the Blue Boar.

On his return to the Blue Boar to cogitate on the clue Bess had given him, he downed two pints. Maken commiserated with the plight of the lovelorn outlaw.

She offered her services. But the handjob from fair Bess had satisfied his morning need.

The next day Robin set out from the Blue Boar to explore Tuxford. He was bedecked in a motley jerkin but was attired below, as always, in his tight tights. He wandered about the hamlet juggling three colored balls. His skill in the art of balancing the colorful balls matched his skill in all he undertook. Pennies were thrown at him by the good dwellers of the hamlet.

"Thank you and God bless," Robin responded as he stooped to pick up each penny that was tossed at his feet.

As he arose from scooping a tuppence, he spied a lovely lass smiling at him. She licked a dab of sweetmeat from her lips. Robin recognized those lips. They belonged to the same brown-haired lass named Dorothy who had lightly kissed each of his cheeks under the Trystell-tree in Sherwood Forest.

Dorothy, at first glance, spied not three balls, but five. Three were being juggled in the air and two were clearly defined within a pair of tight tights.

"Interesting balls you have there, Master Juggler," the lassie taunted him. "All five of them."

"I am delighted they please you," Robin answered gallantly.

"You are a ways from home, are you not, Master Juggler?" the maid queried.

"What makes you say so, Bonnie Lass?" Robin answered.

"The last time I saw you, you were deep in Sherwood Forest under the Great Oak I believe."

"So I was, Dorothy," Robin answered her, showing he remembered her name. "I well remember the pleasure of those cherry lips gracing my cheeks."

The motley juggler, continued with his balancing act.

"Did that truly pleasure you?" the maid asked saucily.

"I'm not quite sure," the juggler responded. "Why don't we give it a try again to determine whether or not it pleasured me," he quipped.

"I, too, would like to check again to make sure," Dorothy agreed.

Dorothy took our hero by the hand and led him to her nearby cottage.

Once there, she engaged him in conversation.

"The rosy cheeks I grazed with my lips belonged to a youth," Dorothy observed. "But he was no juggler in motley. I have since reasoned that he was the infamous outlaw of Sherwood Forest, Master Robin Hood. Would you be he?"

"There is one sure way of finding out," quoth Robin, who removed his motley jerkin and bare-chested stood before her garbed only in Lincoln green tights.

"The suit you wear is somewhat similar to that of Master Robin. But when I first spied him under the oak, he was helplessly a-slumber on the forest floor. So I am not quite sure yet."

Robin removed his tights and exhibiting a brave boner, he sprawled out on the floor of Dorothy's cottage.

The lass bent over him and encircled the entire staff into her moist awaiting mouth.

As she ran her moist mouth up and down his gleeful dick, Robin fondled her ripe hooters.

He had received many a blowjob from Rosalind. But she had only sucked his peckerhead. Dorothy progressed up and down from base to head of the throbbing organ.

Dorothy kept one hand busy entertaining her koozie while slathering the yeoman's pride and joy with her gifted mouth.

Again, both participants climaxed simultaneously.

They then arose, re-clothed themselves, and Dorothy went to her larder as Robin sat at her table.

The lovely lass returned with two pots of ale to the table in the room, and invited Robin to partake of a pot.

"What really brought you to our hamlet, Robin?" she asked sweetly.

"I'll wager you can guess," Robin suggested.

"You would win that wager, Lad," she said. "You are in search of Maid Marian."

"That I am," Robin replied eagerly. "Where does she dwell?"

"That I am sworn not to tell you," Dorothy smiled. "But I can reveal to you the clue she bade me disclose if ever your path crossed mine."

"Tell me, then, Fair Dorothy," Robin urged. "Maid Marian is dear to my heart. And I believe she holds the same loving feeling towards me. What did she tell you to reveal to me?"

"Simply this, Robin," Dorothy confided. "She said to tell you that she dwells in the town where the shadow of your greatest enemy could fall on her any day."

"The shadow of my greatest enemy can fall on her?" Robin pondered. "What does *that* mean?"

"I cannot tell you what it means," answered the maid. "Marian says that if you truly love her you will solve the clues and come into her arms."

Robin realized that all he was going to receive from his encounter with Dorothy other than the memory of the greatest blowjob he could ever imagine was a riddle.

He finished off his ale, arose from the table, kissed the maid gently on her left cheek, and carrying his motley and his juggling balls in his pack and his cudgel in his hand, he left Tuxford for the Lincoln Highway which would lead him back towards the Blue Boar.

As he strode merrily along the dusty highway, a whistle on his lips, a bag in one hand and a cudgel in the other, and a resurrected hardon, he was profoundly conscious that his quest was yet unfulfilled.

He had drunk a pot of ale back in Tuxford, but the dusty road had given rise to a new thirst that required attention.

Despite the awesome cocksucking he had been given, he was horny again.

And Robin knew where that thirst could be quenched.

When he arrived at the Blue Boar, Robin saw a number of jolly fellows at the tables laughing, drinking, and enjoying slabs of bread spread with mine host's fine Stilton cheese.

Robin looked around the crowd to see if there were any he knew or any he might need to avoid. For he was no longer disguised.

Sitting at a table was David of Doncaster, the youngest and fairest of face of all the Merrymen. The handsome youth was of quick intellectual bent. David was sitting with another lad, a stranger to Robin's eyes. The two young

26

men were enjoying mine host's excellent brew. Robin took a seat at a table at a distance from the lads. His business at the moment was two-fold – to slake his thirst and to find a noontime solace in intimate female companionship.

When Maken saw Robin take a seat she hurried right over to his table with a pot of humming ale.

"How are you, today, Fair Robin?" Maken asked. "And how goes your quest?"

"Nice of you to ask, Maken Love," Robin answered. "Truth to tell, my quest has led to naught but veiled clues. And although I got a superb blowjob this morning, I am again in a bad way."

"I am sorry to hear that," Maken answered with a smile on her face and not looking sorry at all. "Would you like me to lace your ale with a touch of brandywine? It is all we have in the way of physic."

"Brandywine would not touch me where I hurt," Robin answered.

"And where is it, then, that our Robin would be hurting?" Maken asked, showing some concern but still smiling.

"The equipment tightly packed in my tights seeks the comfort of a moist cunt, to tell it bluntly," Robin answered, smiling back and with a twinkle in his eye.

"Robin," she said. "There are few woes more doleful to a brash young yeoman like yourself. I have a sure remedy for your ailment. But my physic does not come cheap."

Robin sipped his ale. His throat rejoiced in the comfort it gave to its parched condition. It appeared that his other condition might soon be remedied as well.

"When might you be available to physic my dire condition?" Robin asked.

"That depends," Maken answered.

"It depends on what?"

"On when Mistress Hyacinth can take care of the trade out here at the tables for a spell."

Robin quaffed a mouthful of ale, belched, and then laughed.

"Hie yourself to mine hostess then, Fair Maken. My thirst begins to slake. But my lust still craves a welcoming."

"Wait here, Robin," she counseled. "I will go to the kitchen and see when my mistress can relieve me in serving the stout fellows at the tables."

Maken scurried away inside the inn. The sooner Mistress Hyacinth could relieve Maken the sooner Maken could relieve Robin's need.

Maken was back in a trice.

"My mistress can leave her kitchen now," Maken told her aching customer. "Leave your bag, your cudgel, and your pot of ale here. Come with me. But bring your purse with you."

Behind the inn was a humble shack where Maken plied her second trade. Robin had not been inside the shack before, preferring to find carnal love with damsels who were not of professional bent. But he had always felt some lust for the wench and knew there would eventually be occasions when he would need to pay for her ministrations. He sensed that afternoon would not be his last visit to Maken's shack.

The furnishings inside the shack were simple. A bed, a table, two chairs, a shelf with a jar on it, a wash basin and a pitcher of water. Not so much as a picture was on the wall nor a rug upon the floor. In its simplicity it served its purpose.

Maken stood there looking at him, a merry twinkle in her eye and a bright smile upon her face.

Robin laid his purse on the table, opened it, removed an angel, and laid it on the table's edge. It was exactly the fee Maken exacted for her services. Maken picked up the coin, dropped it in the pot she kept on the shelf as her depository, and snuggled into Robin's arms for a welcoming hug.

Some time later, Robin departed from Maken's shack sporting a jaunty walk and a radiant smile.

His prick had found the comfort of a warm cunt.

Handjobs and blowjobs were all very well. But nothing in life beats a real, honest to God fuck.

In summer time, when leaves grow green,
Down a down a down
And birds sing on every tree,
Hey down a down a down.

Robin Hood went to Nottingham,
Down a down a down
As fast as hee could dree.
Hey down a down a down.

And as hee came to Nottingham
A Tinker he did meet,
And seeing him a lusty blade,
He did him kindly greet.

"Where dost thou live?" quoth Robin Hood,
"I pray thee now mee tell;

Sad news I hear there is abroad,
I fear all is not well."

"What is that news?" the Tinker said;
"Tell mee without delay;
I am a tinker by my trade,
And do live at Banbura."

"As for the news," quoth Robin Hood,
"It is but as I hear;
Two tinkers they were set ith' stocks,
For drinking ale and bear."

"If that be all," the Tinker said,
"As I may say to you,
Your news it is not worth a fart,
Since that they all bee true.

"For drinking of good ale and bear,
You wil lose your part:"
"No, by my faith," quoth Robin Hood,
"I love it with all my heart.

"What news abroad?" quoth Robin Hood;
"Tell mee what thou dost hear;
Being thou goest from town to town,
Some news thou need not fear."

"All the news," the Tinker said,
"I hear, it is for good;
It is to seek a bold outlaw,
Which they call Robin Hood.

"I have a warrant from the king,
To take him where I can;
If you can tell me where hee is,
I will make you a man.

"The king will give a hundred pound
That hee could but him see;
And if wee can but now him get,
It will serve you and mee."

"Let see that warrant," said Robin Hood
"I'le see if it bee right;
And I will do the best I can
For to take him this night."

"That will I not," the Tinker said;
"None with it I will trust;
And where hee is if you'l not tell,
Take him by force I must."

But Robin Hood perceiving well
How then the game would go,
"If you will go to Nottingham,
Wee shall find him I know."

The Tinker had a crab-tree staff,
Which was both good and strong;
Robin hee had a good strong blade,
So they went both along.

And when they came to Nottingham,
There they both tooke one inn;
And they calld for ale and wine,
To drink it was no sin.

But ale and wine they drank so fast
That the Tinker hee forgot,
What thing he was about to do;
It fell so to his lot

That while the Tinker fell asleep,
Hee made then haste away,
And left the Tinker in the lurch,
For the great shot to pay.

But when the Tinker wakened,
And saw that he was gone,
He calld then even for his host,
And thus hee made his moan.

"I had a warrant from the king,
Whichh might have done me good,
That is to take a bold outlaw,

Some call him Robin Hood.

"But now my warrant and mony's gone,
Nothing I have to pay;
And he that promised to be my friend,
He is gone and fled away."

"That friend you tell on," said the host,
"They call him Robin Hood;
And when that first hee met with you,
He ment you little good."

"Had I known it had been hee,
When that I had him here,
Th' one of us should have tri'd our strength
Which should have paid full dear.

"In the mean time I must away;
No longer here I'le bide;
But I will go and seek him out,
What ever do me betide.

"But one thing I would gladly know,
What here I have to pay;"
"Ten shillings just," then said the host;
"I'le pay without delay.

"Or elce take here my working-bag,
And my good hammer too;
And if that I light but on the knave,
I will then soon pay you."

"The onely way," then said the host,
"And not to stand in fear,
Is to seek him among the parks,
Killing of the kings deer."

The Tinker hee then went with speed,
And made then no delay,
Till he had found then Robin Hood,
That they might have a fray.

At last hee spy'd him in a park,

Hunting then of the deer;
"What knave is that," quoth Robin Hood,
"That doth come mee so near?"

"No knave, no knave," the Tinker said,
"And that you soon shall know;
Whether of us hath done most wrong,
My crab-tree staff shall show."

Then Robin drew his gallant blade,
Made then of trusty steel;
But the Tinker laid on him fast
That he made Robin reel.

Then Robins anger did arise;
He fought full manfully,
Until hee made the Tinker
Almost then fit to fly.

With that they had a bout again,
They ply'd their weapons fast;
The Tinker threshed his bones so sore
He made him yeeld at last.

"A boon, a boon," Robin hee cryes,
If thou wilt grant it mee;"
"Before I do it," the Tinker said,
"I'le hang thee on this tree."

But the Tinker looking him about,
Robin his horn did blow;
Then came unto him Little John,
And William Scadlock too.

"What is the matter," quoth Little John,
"You sit in th' highway side?"
"Here is a Tinker that stands by,
That hath paid well my hide."

"That Tinker," then said Little John,
"Fain that blade I would see,
And I would try what I could do,
If hee'l do as much for mee."

But Robin hee then wished them both
They should the quarrel cease,
"That henceforth wee may bee as one,
And ever live in peace.

"And for the jovial Tinker's part,
A hundred pound I'le give,
In th' year to maintain him on,
As long as he doth live.

"In manhood hee is a mettle man,
And a mettle man by trade;
I never thought that any man
Should have made me so fraid.

"And if hee will bee one of us,
Wee will take all one fare,
And whatsoever wee do get,
He shall have his full share."

So the Tinker was content
With them to go along,
And with them a part to take,
And so I end my song.

Child, Francis James, *The English and Scottish Popular Ballads*, Volume III, No. 127

CHAPTER FOUR

The Singing Tinker

Maken, having lavished her Paphian arts to the benefit of the green-clad lad, returned to her serving duties full of her customary dimpled smiles and winks. Robin returned to his table, picked up his pack and cudgel, and proceeded to the table where sat David of Doncaster and his youthful friend.

"May I join you, David?" Robin asked.

"A pleasure, Robin. A pleasure," said the handsome youth.

Robin took a seat.

"My friend Guillaume de Bois-Guilbert," David announced. "Meet my friend and respected leader and master, Robin Hood of Barnsdale and Sherwood Forest."

"I am very honored, My Sir," the young man replied in a very thick Norman accent.

A rotund friar sitting at a nearby table was staring fixedly at David, Guillaume and Robin. Robin was not one to be favorably impressed by abbots, priests, or friars. He had always perceived them as favoring the privileged classes against the poor. He felt they tended to have more interest in earthly treasures than in its heavenly counterpart. But he was not close-minded enough to shun individual churchmen. And the inquisitive friar was of jolly mien. On a whim, Robin beckoned him to come join their table. The jolly friar picked up his pot of ale, brought it to David's table, and sat.

"I would give you a blessing," the jolly friar said with a chuckle. "But anyone sitting under Master Eadom's oak is already blessed quite enough. Would you not agree?"

The greeting pleased Robin well. Here was a friar after his own heart.

Maken appeared at the table.

"Good yeomen and friar," she beamed. "Are you well taken care of?"

Robin smiled his broadest smile at her.

"Maken, Love. You have truly taken care of me well."

He smirked at her and she winked back.

"But," he continued, "my friends and I do have a persistent thirst. Another pot of ale each, and add it to my score."

"Thank you, Sweet Robin," Maken replied and skipped off to take care of the order.

Maken was soon back with the brews. The friar, the Norman youth, David, and Robin engaged in merry conversation.

Seated at a central table under the spreading oak sat a tinker. He wore his bell about his neck. His pack was to his left, with his tinker hammer and a hand harp affixed to its surface. His crab-tree staff rested to his right.

The itinerant tradesman arose and jingled the bell that was his tinker's hallmark.

"Good yeomen, squires, merchants, pilgrims, and God's creatures all," he said in resonant voice. "I, an itinerant tinker, bring my abundant skills to serve the good people of Nottinghamshire.

"Among my skills I possess a goodly voice and know scores of ballads, songs and ditties gleaned from my travels throughout the lanes that grace Good King Harry's lands."

He took his hat off his head and waved it in the air.

"I would regale you with song if your ears would receive it happily..."

The inn's customers clapped and shouted.

"...and generously," the tinker continued. "If you find pleasure in my performance, my hat would joyfully receive tokens of your appreciation."

The tinker placed his hat on the table in position to receive monetary recompense from his audience. He untied the harp from his pack and strummed it three strokes.

Robin and his tablemates leaned back, alepots in hand. They prepared to enjoy whatever entertainment the tinker might provide.

With a clear, sweet voice the tinker rendered his song:

Back and side go bare, go bare,
Both hand and foot go cold.
But, belly, God send thee good ale enough
Whether it be new or old.

But if that I may truly have
Good ale my belly full,

I shall look like one, by sweet Saint John,
Were shorn against the wool.
Though I go bare, take ye no care,
I am nothing a-cold.
I stuff my skin so full within
Of jolly good ale and old.

I cannot eat but little meat,
My stomach is not good.
But sure I think that I could drink
With him that weareth an hood.
Drink is my life, although my wife
Some time do chide and scold,
Yet spare I not to ply the pot.
Of jolly good ale and old.

I love no roast but a brown toast,
Or a crab in the fire.
A little bread shall do me stead,
Much bread I ne'er desire.
Nor frost, nor snow, nor wind, I trow,
Can hurt me if it wolde.
I am so wrapped within, and lapped
With jolly good ale and old.

I care right naught, I take no thought
For clothes to keep me warm.
Have I good drink, I surely think
Nothing can do me harm.
For truly than I fear no man,
Be he never so bold,
When I am armed and thoroughly warmed
With jolly good ale and old.

But now and than I curse and ban,
They make their ale so small!
God give them care, and evil to fare!
They strye the malt and all.
Such peevish pew, I tell you true,
Not for a crown of gold
There cometh one sip within my lip,
Whether it be new or old.

Good ale and strong maketh me among
Full jocund and full light,
That oft I sleep, and take no keep
From morning until night.
Then start I up and flee to the cup,
The right way on I hold.
My thirst to stanch I fill my paunch
With jolly good ale and old.

And Kit, my wife, that as her life
Loveth well good ale to seek,
Full oft drinketh she that ye may see
The tears run down her cheek.
Then doth she troll to me the bowl
As a good mall-worm should,
And say, "Sweetheart, I take my part
Of jolly good ale and old."

They that do drink till they nod and wink,
Even as good fellows should do,
They shall not miss to have the bliss
That good ale hath brought them to.
And all poor souls that scour black bowls,
And hath them lustily troll'd,
God save the lives of them and their wives,
Whether they be young or old!

Back and side go bare, go bare,
Both hand and foot go cold.
But, belly, God send the good ale enough
Whether it be new or old.

Robin's companions agreed that the tinker sang sweet and true. Guillaume did not quite understand all the English words, but his Norman heart rejoiced in the music itself.

Robin noted that while the tinker sang his song, David of Doncaster's left hand was resting friskily on Guillaume de Bois-Guilbert's codpiece. And, in reciprocation, the Norman's right hand had found similar refuge on David's lap above a palpitation beneath his tights.

Robin was open-minded about the personal preferences of his men, yet smiled at the open admiration the two showed for the other's laps in the open under the spreading oak.

The tinker circulated through the crowd and coins filled his hat thrice over.

When the tinker returned to his pack for the last time to fill it with the coins he had collected, Robin bethought himself to join him and see what manner of man the sweet-voiced one was.

Robin approached the tinker's table.

"A timely and well-sung song, Master Tinker," Robin congratulated him. "May I order a pot of ale for each of us?"

"Thank you, good yeoman," replied the tinker. "Pray be seated. I would drink lustily with any man who relishes a merry Saxon tune."

Maken, ever aware of her customers' whims and needs, was at tableside immediately. She took the order and was shortly back with two pots of the inn's finest brown October ale.

"Jolly good ale and old," Robin toasted the singing tinker.

The tinker sipped.

"Jolly good indeed," he exclaimed. "You must be a favorite of this house to merit such tasty brew."

"I dwell nearby, and am not unknown to mine hosts and the lusty serving wench," Robin said. "Tinkers aplenty come down this highway and stop to enjoy a pot at the Blue Boar. But never have I heard so fair a voice from the brothers in your trade. I see your voice serves your well-filled hat."

"I am a man who is lively for a penny, a shilling, an angel, or a pound," the tinker replied. "I serve those who can use a man with tinker's skills, Saxon voice, or crab-tree staff. I serve those who are not shy of paying well. This very day I have a very special service for a high placed gentleman."

"What special service do you bear within your pack today, Master Tinker?" Robin inquired.

"The noble Sheriff of Nottingham has entrusted me with a very special duty."

Robin's interest was aroused. The Sheriff of Nottingham was his sworn enemy. It was the sheriff's threat that he would see Robin hanged where three roads meet. Any duty the sheriff entrusted to anyone, tinker, constable, or merchant, was worth Robin's attention.

"You are a special envoy of our beloved sheriff?" Robin asked. "You are honored indeed. With what function has he entrusted you?"

"No one in Nottingham Town was man enough to serve the king's own warrant upon a certain errant knave," the tinker answered. "I have no fear of any man and agreed to carry in my pouch a warrant for the arrest of the greatest blackguard in the entire shire. I shall serve it on the varlet and if he resists I will beat him to a hasty pudding, drag him by a leash to Nottingham Town and deliver him to the sheriff in the name of good King Harry."

"You are a stout fellow," Robin told him. "Who is this villain you seek? If he hails from these parts perhaps I can assist you on your way."

"The man is known as Robin Hood of Locksley Hall," the tinker proudly proclaimed. "He dwells in the woods hereabouts with a ruffian crew. Neither he nor his scurvy band respect the king's law or the sheriff's authority."

"I know who you mean," Robin told him. "The man is a scoundrel indeed and justly deserves the wrath of king and sheriff. Are you sure the warrant is fully legal and valid?"

"Oh, it is," replied the tinker. "It is written very prettily on parchment and is held in place with a great red seal."

"Let me see that warrant," Robin asked. "I know a bit about these things and can determine whether the warrant is legal in these parts."

"That I cannot do, though I esteem you, young man," was the tinker's response. "No one shall see it until I serve it on that scamp and give him a rightful buffet on the pate with my trusty cudgel as well."

"What will it earn you when you have served our noble sheriff in this manner?" Robin inquired.

"A reward, my friend. A reward," the tinker declared. "The king will give me a hundred pounds when I have served the warrant and dragged the wretch to jail."

"A hundred pounds is a pretty sum," said Robin, remembering what he had recently purchased in Maken's shack for a price of but one angel.

"Do I understand that you know the criminal?" the tinker asked.

"Indeed I do," quoth Robin. "He dwells in the forest hereabouts and comes often to this very potshop. In fact, I saw him this very morning sitting saucily at that table over there."

"What does the blackguard look like?" asked the tinker.

"Not unlike me," Robin answered. "About my height, weight, and coloring. He has reddish yellow hair and beard, blue eyes, and is sturdily built. I find him brash of manner. And he is given to wearing suits of Lincoln green."

"Like the jerkin and tights you are wearing," observed the tinker.

Robin looked down at his clothing as though noticing the color for the first time.

"You are right, Friend Tinker. I guess I'd never noticed or thought about that before. He's a sly one, stranger. Beware or he just might steal that warrant right out of your pouch."

"Oh, let him try," boasted the tinker. "Just let him try. I will swing my cudgel onto his wicked pate and reduce him to a bag of bones if he so much as attempts to outsmart Wat of Branbury."

Robin excused himself, claiming he needed to relieve himself of the excess ale that burdened his bladder.

"Do not leave until I return," he said. "On my way to the privy I will instruct the saucy serving wench to bring us pots of a special brew that mine host reserves only for his favored guests. If you were not sitting with me, you would never have had the chance to taste the finest brew in seven shires."

The tinker remained steadfast in his seat until his newfound friend returned.

Robin entered the inn and found Master Eadom.

"Master Eadom," he said. "When I return to my table, send Maken out with two pots of October Ale. Lace one of them with strong brandywine. Be sure Maken serves that one to the tinker. The other have her serve me. That varlet out there serves the sheriff who has entrusted the knave with the king's own warrant for my arrest. And as we know the sheriff would see my neck stretched tight where three roads meet."

"Trust me, Fair Robin," said mine host. "The villain shall have his head resting on the table within the hour."

Robin proceeded to the rear of the inn, to the privy that was situated well beyond Maken's shack. When he had pissed out the brew his bladder stored he returned to the table.

No sooner was he seated than Maken brought two pots to the table. One she carefully placed before Wat the Tinker. The other before Robin. She could not resist bestowing a knowing wink on her current favorite customer.

"By Our Lady," claimed the tinker. "That is the finest ale ever I tasted."

"Drink up," Robin encouraged. "You may not have the chance to quaff such stuff again for a long time."

The tinker downed a second cup and began to sing:

Old Grahame he is to Carlisle gone,
Where Sir Robert Bewich there met he;
In arms to the brandywine they are gone,
And drank till they were both merry.

"Have another pot, good Wat of Banbura," Robin urged. "It loosens up your voice.

Wat interrupted his song.

"I will, I will." And he downed still another pot of the brandywine laced ale.

Old Grahame he took up the cup,
And said, "Brother Bewich, here's to thee,
And here's to our two sons at home.
For they live best in our country."

As that verse was drawing to a close the tinker's head sank closer and closer to the table. And on the last word he had passed out sound asleep.

Merry Robin took the tinker's pouch in hand, opened it, and extracted the document. He carried it to David's table.

"Here, my friend, is a warrant from our king, dispatched through the Sheriff of Nottingham, inviting me to a hanging. What say you, Friar? Do you have a blessing for a hanging?"

Friar Tuck, for that was the worthy's name, gave the matter some consideration.

He read the warrant.

"I see that the warrant is for the arrest and hanging of the outlaw Robin Hood. I cannot give it a blessing."

"Why not, Friar?" asked Robin.

"Because that particular outlaw cannot be hanged."

"And why is that?" Robin asked.

"Because there is ample testimony from every damsel and goodwife in the shire who has marveled at what is clearly visible within his tight, tight tights, that Robin Hood is already hung," replied the jolly friar.

There was no doubt that David of Doncaster had already apprised Friar Tuck about who Robin was.

The friar's response caused Robin and David to laugh heartily. The jest was lost on Guillaume's Norman wit.

"What shall we do then with this worthless document?" Robin wondered.

"Since it is worthless, why not cut it to handy size and send it to the privy?" suggested Friar Tuck. "As it happens, I have a great urge to relieve my bowels. I would be most happy to undertake the task of supplying parchment wipes for the shitty arseses of the guests of the Blue Boar."

With his trusty dirk, Robin cut the warrant into hand-sized sheets. Friar Tuck arose, and proceeded to the privy behind the inn.

And that is how the next few guests of the Blue Boar to use the privy enjoyed the luxury of wiping their butts with the gloriously soft parchment of the sheriff's warrant.

Robin went inside the inn to talk to Master Eadom.

"Mine host," he said. "I have been the guest and table companion of the singing tinker who dozes outside. He and I have drunk well of your humming ale. I am about to depart. Will you see to it that my friend the tinker pays the score? He has earned ample from his singing to take care of the matter many times over."

Master Eadom enjoyed the jest. And he assured Robin that the tinker would indeed pay the score.

"And if he resists?" asked Robin.

"Our good friend Brian always makes sure our guests never shirk paying their score," mine host chuckled. "Do they, Brian?"

At hearing his master say his name the mastiff raised his eyes. Robin could swear the dog actually smiled.

Robin bid adieu to David, Friar Tuck, and Guillaume and proceeded down the dusty highway.

As David stood to wish his leader well, Robin noticed that his young follower's tights were heavily spotted at the crotch with what clearly appeared to be jism.

David looked down at the spot and smiled.

He declared to Robin and the friar, "You will have to excuse me. I seem to have spilled some ale on myself."

Robin departed and went on down the road smiling too broadly to be able to whistle his merry tune.

He was in no rush, so, as was his wont, he stopped along the way to chat with fellow travelers. In that way he kept himself apprised of what was current news in Good King Henry's kingdom. And even of the news from far beyond.

He learned that Prince Richard, known as the Lion-Hearted, was planning on leaving England to go on Crusade to the Holy Land. Robin was concerned, since, if King Henry should die, and Prince Richard should be out of the country, that would leave England to be ruled by Prince John. Robin knew well that the yeomen of England, and the Merrymen in particular, would not fare well under a King John.

Even though King Harry had issued a warrant for his arrest, the sovereign was more favorably disposed towards the yeomen of his realm than was Prince John. And good Prince Richard of the Lion's Heart was known to have a sympathetic view of his Saxon compatriots.

Back at the inn, the tinker awoke from his doze. The first thing he noticed was that his pouch was open on the table. He looked inside and found the warrant gone. He swore a mighty oath and demanded that those at nearby tables tell him who the thief was who had robbed him of his warrant.

It seemed that no one knew a thing about it. But each ale drinker seemed somewhat amused as he proclaimed his ignorance.

The tinker looked about to find his former table companion. He asked if anyone knew where the young man was.

"Oh, the handsome youth dressed in Lincoln green?" answered one of the guests. "He left not long ago. I saw him head down the highway whistling the very tune you sang just as you were falling into your nap."

The tinker's face turned red. He pounded the table. He began to suspect who his table companion had been and he was determined to chase after him, beat him with his crab-tree staff, and haul his body back to Nottingham.

Wat of Banbura, for such was the name he had given at the table, grabbed his staff and his pack, preparing to pursue the robber. But Master Eadom stood in his way.

"Your score, fair tinker, is ten shillings."

"I was the guest of that scurvy knave who robbed me of a warrant in my pouch," the tinker objected. "He must pay the score. Not I."

"Your friend has left," replied Master Eadom. "He told me you would pay. I will not be cheated of my ten shillings. I know you have earned many times that amount while a guest at my table. Pay me you must."

Wat the Tinker shook his staff at the host.

"I will not pay for pots drunk by the man who robbed me. I am off to catch him and give him a taste of my staff. Do not stand in my way or you will receive a taste of this sturdy staff yourself."

Master Eadom whistled into the wind. And within seconds Brian was at his side snarling at Wat.

No one with an ounce of sense would argue with the teeth displayed in Brian's maw.

Grudgingly, the tinker paid the host and departed hastily down the highway in pursuit of Robin Hood.

David of Doncaster and his two table companions watched the exchange between Master Eadom and Wat of Branbury. Friar Tuck became so amused at the scene that his chuckles fairly burst from him. David laughed also, but not as boisterously as the friar. Guillaume de Bois-Guilbert's English was insufficient to follow the proceedings but he smiled politely nonetheless.

Robin had already paid the score for the three so they were free to leave.

"Let us follow the knave and see what sport ensues when he again meets Robin face-to-face," David suggested.

"I would not miss it for a crown in Heaven," Friar Tuck agreed.

Before arising, Friar Tuck made a sign of the cross over the splotch on David's crotch, which elicited a blush from the young outlaw.

Guillaume de Bois-Guilbert had observed a lad who had recently arrived at the Blue Boar. The youth had the manner of a Norman and was clothed in the livery of a Norman page. Guillaume was much more interested in joining a fellow Norman for a glass of whatever wine or cider the host might serve than accompany his Saxon-speaking drinking companions. Thus, he stayed behind, bidding adieu to his recent tablemates.

But as he stood, he pulled his velvet jacket firmly down over his codpiece. For it was besmirched in like fashion to David's tights.

The friar and the yeoman set out to follow the angry tinker to see what might befall him down the highway.

On the road, Robin was in earnest conversation with an itinerant wine merchant who was on his way to Barnsdale. Robin was not much of a wine drinker, but he gathered as much information as he could about any commerce that flowed up and down the Lincoln Highway. A good robber has need of good intelligence.

Robin spied a robust hart leaping through the adjacent forest. He took leave of the wine merchant and stepped into the greenwood with an arrow nocked to his bowstring.

He was aimed and poised to shoot when his aim was deflected by a voice from behind. It was that of the tinker.

"I am right happy to see you again, Master Tinker," Robin said. "Apparently you enjoy my company enough to come pay me a visit closer to my forest neighborhood. Be assured you are welcome."

"You will welcome my staff on your thieving pate," the tinker replied. "I believe you are that rascal Robin Hood. You stole your warrant right out from under my nose."

"Did I not warn you that the outlaw might do something like that"? Robin asked. "You should have heeded my warning."

"Then you admit you are Robin of Locksley Hall?" Watt demanded.

"At your service," replied Robin.

"Then I will beat you to a pulp with my good staff," said the tinker. "And I will haul your scrawny arse to Nottingham Town where the sheriff will hang what is left of you as warning to all that your likes will not be tolerated in this fair shire."

"I invited you to try to attack me, Wat of Branbury," Robin taunted. He set his bow on the ground and readied his cudgel. "As I mentioned, I am entirely at your service."

David of Doncaster and Friar Tuck had caught up with the scene, entered the greenwood, and watched the proceedings from a distance.

The tinker was no mean master of his staff. He swung it with more force than would have been expected from a man his size.

Robin parried the blow with a resounding whack and managed to give his opponent a glancing blow on his left shoulder.

Tinker Wat was not one to show discomfort and whirled his staff around catching Robin a blow to his butt that nearly knocked the green-clad youth to the ground.

Staff to cudgel the two men fought, neither apparently able to gain fair advantage over the other.

Wat gave a sharp buffet with his staff to which Robin attempted a parry of his cudgel. But although Robin's cudgel was hewn from sturdy oak, it shattered from the blow. Robin appeared to be defenseless against the angered tinker and David and Friar Tuck feared the tinker would now be able to heap blows on Robin that would either kill or maim him.

Robin, aware of his vulnerability, asked the tinker, "A boon. A boon."

"No boon for you, Knave," the tinker replied. "I will see you hanged first, as the king's stolen warrant decrees."

In desperation Robin raised his horn to his lips and managed to blow thrice thereon while executing some lively steps to avoid the tinker's staff and wrath.

At the sound of the third blast Littlejohn and Will Scarlet sprang out of the woods. Littlejohn clasped the tinker about the waist whilst Will disarmed him.

"What happened here?" Littlejohn inquired of his chief.

"That tinker you hold in close caress came close to tanning my hide, and has come to haul my arse to the Sheriff of Nottingham to get me hanged," Robin answered.

"Is that so?" replied Littlejohn. "Then for his troubles we will repay him by stretching his neck on a rope hanging from a sturdy bough of the Great Oak."

"Not so," said Robin. "He is a fighter worth his salt. He was to receive the king's bounty of a hundred pounds. I will pay him that much myself for his trouble. And, to boot, he sings a fair and merry tune."

Robin addressed the tinker.

"You are a man of great determination. You fight with a fierce intensity that pleases me. And we have no singer to supply minstrelsy to our band. If you will forswear allegiance to the sheriff, we will welcome you to join our merry crew."

Littlejohn let loose his firm grasp from around the tinker's waist.

Robin continued.

"If you would throw in your lot with us, I offer you not only the hundred pounds King Harry promised, but three jerkins and tights of Lincoln green, forty marks in fee, and the privilege of sharing all we have. And what is more, living among us as one of us, you will lead a merry life in the greenwood."

Wat stood straight and tall and looked Robin in the eye.

"Your offer is one that pleases me well," he affirmed. "I love a merry life. And I favor a man who shows good wit and a crafty temperament. With all my heart I will join your band of merry men."

David of Doncaster approached with Friar Tuck. He joined in the celebration of the newly admitted member of the band.

While watching the proceedings, Friar Tuck had indicated that he also would lief join the band.

"Robin," David said. "You have drunk with this good friar and have laughed at his merry japes. He would join our band and can provide much sport for us with his ready wit. What say you?"

Robin had taken a great liking to the jolly friar and welcomed him on the spot.

"We herewith add two more to our band of sevenscore. You, tinker, if I recall aright, are called Wat of Branbury."

"I have trod the highways of the kingdom under that name," the man said. "But to you I can tell the truth. I am a merry minstrel of the North Country yclept Allan a Dale. Up in my home shire I killed a Norman knight, Sir Stephen Fitzknee, who had sported with my lemman[3], Alisoun o' Blairgowrie against her will. I have been on the run ever since in the guise of a tinker with the simple name of Wat, and with a price on my head."

Robin answered, "Then here amongst us you shall be known by your true name, Allan a Dale[4], and shall fill our ears with merry songs of an evening."

"Then I join your band gladly," responded the new recruit. "And I will lend my voice to all the mirth that Robin Hood and his Merrymen enjoy in Sherwood Forest."

"And as for you," Robin addressed the rotund friar. "Your name, Friar Tuck, suits you well. And thus you shall remain named in our jolly crew."

The band proceeded into the forest and the newly acquired members were introduced and accepted by all.

The Merrymen volunteered to help Friar Tuck and Allan a Dale construct huts and cots for themselves. Allan was handier with a hammer, knife, saw and ax than any of the band and built his own hut and cot unassisted.

Friar Tuck scarcely knew a hammer from a saw, but so amused the Merrymen with his wit that they constructed a hut for him without his physical assistance.

And thus the band's size was increased by two members.

And while the new members were being busily welcomed into the band, David of Doncaster was down at Clough Creek, busily scrubbing the cum out of his tights.

---

3   Sweetheart or mistress.

4   Scholars believe Allan a Dale was, historically, a twelfth century minstrel and balladeer who composed and sang lays about the folk hero, Robin Hood. The excerpted lay on pages 36-38 and 80-81 is said to be typical of Allan a Dale's style.

CHAPTER FIVE

A Lover's Quest

The Sheriff of Nottingham was not a popular man in his shire. The affluent and influential subjects within his bailiwick were upset because he was not able to capture and punish the notorious outlaw of Sherwood Forest who robbed from them and gave to the poor. The poor and downtrodden were partisans of Robin and his band and were opposed to the sheriff's animosity towards their hero.

The sheriff argued that his staff of fourscore officers was considerably smaller than Robin's band of sevenscore.

He decided to go to London Town for an audience with King Henry and Queen Eleanor. Perhaps, if he made an urgent enough appeal, the royals would dispatch an army unit to Nottinghamshire and roust the blackguards out of their forest refuge and the sheriff's men could then capture them and hang a few.

The royal audience was granted. The sheriff proceeded to London Town with a dozen of his most imposing looking officers.

To King Henry, the sheriff emphasized that the outlaw band was poaching on the royal deer. A capital offense. To Queen Eleanor, he emphasized that Robin had murdered a stalwart forester who was loyal to the state. Another capital offense.

Henry II had ruled England for thirty-two years. In addition to being sovereign of that great kingdom he was hereditary Count of Anjou and Duke of Normandy. Thus his domain was one of the greatest in Europe. He loved a good fight and he enjoyed female companionship. A more ribald monarch was not to be found in Christendom. He deplored weakness and had no respect for a sniveling sheriff who came crying for someone to do a job that was his sole responsibility.

Queen Eleanor was as lusty as her husband. Eleanor of Aquitaine, in addition to being Queen of England, was hereditary Duchess of the Aquitaine, the most fertile province on the continent. She had been previously married to King Louis VII of France and had accompanied him on the Second Crusade to the Holy Land. She rode across all Europe bare-breasted and took a different young soldier to her bed every night. King Louis was not aware of her adultery until the couple returned to France. He divorced her.

Eleanor then married Henry of Anjou who became King of England in 1154.

Eleanor continued to take young men to her bed. And her husband, Henry, was so busy wenching that he did not object if she did not complain about his love life.

Both King Henry and Queen Eleanor had heard many a tale and much jocund minstrelsy about the outlaws of Barnsdale and Sherwood Forest and their brave, handsome, young leader, Robin Hood. King Henry admired the outlaw's spunk and bravery. Eleanor wanted to test the young man's virility.

If the tales circulating about the size and athleticism of his prick were true, she would love to offer that member the services of her royal mouth, hands, and hearty cunt and arse.

In short, the queen admired the outlaw much more than did her husband.

So although the king merely dismissed the sheriff as incompetent, Eleanor offered to give him double the two hundred pounds reward if he could deliver Robin, unharmed, to her personal suite in the royal palace.

The sheriff returned to Nottingham feeling he had made a fool of himself. The king's ire was apparent. And he believed the queen's offer of the high bounty was insincere -- a joke leveled at him personally.

The sheriff was determined to catch that caitiff rascal Robin Hood and deliver him to Queen Eleanor. He would also flush out the tinker who had defected and hang him high where three roads meet. Then, he would make short work of the remaining sevenscore devils who dwelt in Sherwood Forest.

The sheriff pondered how to catch Robin Hood without the help of additional men from the royal couple.

An idea came to him. Aha! It was known that Robin Hood took great pride in his bowmanship. Catch a thief by playing on his boastfulness and vanity.

The sheriff told his henchmen his idea.

"I will institute a shooting match, set for Saint Willibald's day next" he proclaimed. "Saint Willibald, being a Saxon, a great bowman, and an enemy of the Saracen, will irresistibly draw the hotblooded outlaw of Sherwood Forest into our clutches. It will be the most prestigious contest in all the kingdom. We will send heralds throughout the land, to every town, hamlet, and countryside, proclaiming the event. I will have a valuable arrow made by our finest goldsmith and our most renowned silversmith. It will be an arrow of the purest beaten gold and silver. That will flush merry Robin into my waiting hands when his arrogance drives him to participate in our archery contest. What say you, men?"

The sheriff's flunkies fell all over themselves in praise of their leader's great idea. What a wonderful scheme. A trap!

Robin was enjoying a pot of ale at the Blue Boar with a dozen of his Merrymen when one of the heralds sent throughout the realm arrived and made the announcement of the contest.

Will Scarlet was excited by the news.

"With that prize of the gold and silver arrow, we will have the best archers in England coming to our shire. I would dearly love to see Gilbert o' the Red Cap compete. He's the best bowman in the kingdom."

Arthur a Bland did not agree.

"Gilbert can draw a fine bow. But for my money Hubert o' Cloud is the better man. If they both compete nothing can keep me from going to Nottingham Town to see which of the two wins the arrow. But I would wager on Hubert."

"Our leader, Robin, could best the two of them twice over," answered Will. "No man in the kingdom draws a prettier bow."

"Do you suppose he'll compete?" Arthur asked.

Littlejohn had held his peace until then. He now spoke up.

"I smell a trap in all this," he declared. "Why do you think this contest is being heralded all of a sudden? I think it's the sheriff's doing. The only reason for an archery contest with a big prize in Nottingham Town is to lure our Robin and trap him."

Robin had been sitting at the next table and overheard the discussion. He came over to Will Scarlet's table.

Littlejohn appealed to Robin.

"Did you hear our discussion, Robin?"

"I overheard it, yes."

"What think you?" Littlejohn asked. "These men would like to see you participate in the contest, but I sense a trap."

"I would love to match bows with the likes of Adam o' the Dell, on Saint Willibald's Day next," Robin answered. "I know myself to be the finest bowman in Nottinghamshire. I've never been able to test my mettle against England's greats. But, much as I would love the competition, I believe Littlejohn is right. I think the sheriff is behind all this. And the prize he's hoping to bestow on me is a public hanging."

No one argued with Robin. If he sensed a trap, it would be foolish of him to enter the contest. That ended the discussion.

The following morning, back in the greenwood, Robin appeared dejected. Many of his men felt that he was moping because he wanted to compete for the gold and silver arrow but didn't feel it was safe to do so. Others thought there was more behind his funk than that, because they thought he had been in a poor mood even before the herald had brought the announcement to the Blue Boar.

Friar Tuck and David of Doncaster were concerned about Robin. They decided to talk to him, find out what was really bothering him, and help if they could.

They sat down to break their fast with their leader under the Trystell-tree. They asked him why he had been mumpish, and he told them quite frankly.

"I am lovestruck," Robin confided. "My one true love dwells out there somewhere in the wide world, and I cannot find her. I fear I shall be melancholy until I can hold her in my arms and satisfy the longing I know she holds for the prick she grazed under a mighty oak on May Day last."

"Have you no idea whatsoever where the damsel can be found?" Friar Tuck asked.

"She has left me two clues," Robin admitted. "But the more I puzzle over them the more depressed I become. I can derive no meaning at all from the mysterious words her friends have revealed to me."

"What are the words?" David of Doncaster asked. "Perhaps we can help."

"Yes," agreed the friar. "David is a very wizard when it comes to words. I often think he has more words than wit."

David did not seem to know whether his friend was complimenting or joshing him. Knowing Friar Tuck, it was probably the latter. The friar enjoyed a good quip, especially if it was at the expense of a friend. He was a very curious friar.

Robin told them, "One of her friends was able to inform me that Maid Marian lives at the end of the lane."

"Maid Marian," David repeated. "A fair name for a fair damsel. Tell us which lane she lives at the end of and we can work from there."

"That is the problem," Robin answered. "The lass who gave me that clue was not at liberty to reveal anything more."

"The question must have a logical answer," pondered Friar Tuck. "I suppose you believe your Maid Marian truly desires you to find her?"

"Oh, I am quite sure of that," Robin affirmed. "She made it abundantly clear that I am to her taste. No damsel who has once breathed on my dick and then traced its awesome outline when concealed within my tight tights can truly resist me for long."

Friar Tuck and David of Doncaster exchanged meaningful glances but did not comment on Robin's statement.

"In that case," said David, "she meant you to solve the puzzle concerning which lane. Is it likely that she lives in our shire or at least in one of the adjacent ones?"

"Yes," said Robin. "Her friends live nearby. And I met her as she was Maying in Sherwood Forest."

"Then I would guess," said David, "that she must be referring to the most obvious lane in the area. If I were to ask you what lane, road, or highway comes first to your mind, what would you answer?"

"The King's Highway that leads from Nottingham to Lincoln, of course," said Robin. "By Saint George and his dragon, I *do* believe my love dwells at the end of the Lincoln Highway."

"There you have your answer," said Friar Tuck, and acted as though he was prepared to walk away.

"Wait," said Robin. "A problem remains. Which end of the highway is she referring to?"

"Let us think," Friar Tuck said in mock seriousness. "What constitutes the two ends of the highway? I cannot remember for the life of me. What does the King's Highway connect?"

"Why, it goes from Nottingham Town to Lincoln Town," Robin replied.

"There you have it, Robin," David said. "Your Maid Marian dwells either in Nottingham Town or in Lincoln Town. Come, Tuck. Robin has solved his puzzle and can now find the woman he loves."

David and Friar Tuck arose as though preparing to depart.

"Wait, wait," Robin requested. "I must know which town she lives in."

"Do you have another clue?" asked David, resuming his place at the breakfast table.

"Yes," quoth Robin. "The second, and only other clue, is a mystery indeed. She let it be known to me through a friend that she dwells where my worst enemy's shadow can fall on her."

"My, my," David said, wonderingly. But he, of course, had fathomed the answer to the riddle. "Your worst enemy. Who might that be? Let me think. Perhaps it is Sultan Saladin the infidel ruler of the Holy Land. What think you, Tuck?"

Friar Tuck pondered. "No, no. Not Saladin. I'll vouch it is the Devil himself. For we all know Robin to be an egregious sinner."

Robin knew he was being teased and put a stop to it by his declaration.

"Stop, you two zanies. It is obvious to me now. My worst enemy is the Sheriff of Nottingham."

"And where might Maid Marian be if the sheriff's shadow could fall on her?"

Robin burst out laughing.

"Observe," said Friar Tuck to David. "We have our merry Robin with us again. And I'll warrant you he will soon be off to meet his Maid Marian belly to belly at the end of the lane where a certain shadow befouls the dust of the earth."

Robin gave a playful buffet to the two who had led him to the solution of the problem that had rendered him melancholy. He would be off to Nottingham Town to find his true love and garner the yearned for right of entry directly into her cunt.

Robin Hood was possibly the foremost master of disguise in the shire. Or perhaps in the kingdom. He disguised himself as a blind beggar in order to roam the lanes of Nottingham Town in search of the woman who had won his heart. A wide-brimmed hat all but covered his face. A long gray beard covered his lower face. His coat of shreds and patches was enough to arouse pity in the meanest burger. His staff, while appearing fragile, was of sturdy blackthorn that could serve him well if he had need of protection. Stowed beneath the ragged coat, he had tucked away his razor-sharp dirk. He hoped he would not have to draw blood. But if need be, he knew himself to be as handy with a dirk as any yeoman in the shire. He had dispatched three wild boars with it in the forest. No flabby city-dweller would be as fierce a contestant.

His beggar's bowl was an unraveling wicker basket. The cloth within the basket, however, was colored Lincoln green to match his tights. Robin enjoyed the sport of displaying a mirthful clue for his enemies.

In his disguise, Robin entered Nottingham Town.

He stumbled about the high street, stopping from time to time to collect alms and to overhear gossip. He was the recipient of more gossip than pennies. Fortunately for Robin, intelligence about either his love or his enemy was all the riches he sought.

There was much talk in the town of the coming archery match. Gamblers were wagering heavily on the favorites who had already entered the lists. Although Robin did not intend to participate, he imagined what a lark it would be to best the likes of Gilbert o' the Red Cap right under the sheriff's eyes. Nearly irresistible. But he realized it would be absolute folly to appear.

Robin spoke as little as possible in his masquerade. He thought it would be a more effective guise if he appeared mute as well as blind.

A passing bakerboy dropped a scone into his bowl. Robin thought that might be all the sustenance he would receive all day in Nottingham Town, so broke his silence enough to thank the lad.

Outside the Rose and Thistle Tavern at the main crossroads of the town, three boisterous, overweight, staggering men stumbled about. By their attire it was clear all three were constables of the sheriff. They ignored the blind beggar, so absorbed were they in their inebriated chatter.

"Our sheriff is a crafty one," said the stoutest of the three. "The trap he has set will surely snag the fucking bastard."

Robin had no doubt who the "fucking bastard" was. He was right there within reach of the law.

"I'm not so sure," said the tallest of the three. "It is my belief that the asshole is a coward at heart and will not dare to show his craven face in town."

That one smarted. Robin would gladly have given a good whack to the fellow's pate. Coward indeed. He would show...

As irked as Robin was by the drunk's slur, he disciplined himself to hold his peace. He was not a coward. But neither was he a fool.

"I just wish he would show up here," said the third constable. "I'd make him dance a merry step before we hauled his scabby arse up onto the gibbet to provide entertainment for our good burgers."

With a round of drunken laughter the three proceeded up the high street while Robin turned down a modest side lane.

About a half-hour later Robin was stumbling along through the neighborhood when he observed the same drunken constables swaggering towards him. They were laughing boisterously with the type of mirth occasioned by a morning of alcoholic indulgence.

"Ahoy!" blurted the gruffest voiced constable. "A blind beggar. Methinks I saw the scoundrel lurking outside the Rose and Thistle."

"You didn't see a fucking thing outside the tavern," the short one answered. "You were as blind drunk as that pitiful beggar over there."

The third lawman added, "Whether you saw the blind stranger before or not, we have his number here on a side lane where none can interfere if we have a bit of sport with him."

That did not sound like good news to Robin. He felt inside his tattered robe to be absolutely sure that his razor sharp dirk was in place. He gave a thud to the ground with his blackthorn staff to assure himself of its heft. He did not wish to engage in a fight with the sheriff's men. He was willing to take a great deal of abuse to maintain his disguise so he could pursue his quest for his sweetheart. So he braced himself for the unpleasantness which was sure to come.

The fattest constable purposely bumped into Robin, knocking him against the nearby building.

"Out of our way, old man," he shouted in Robin's ear. "Don't you have any respect for the king's law?"

Robin held his peace, but he also stealthily reached towards his dirk.

The constable shouted his stale-breathed voice into Robin's ear.

"I asked you something, you pathetic freak," he shrieked. "Don't you have any respect for Good King Harry's law?" He gave Robin a punch in the belly. *"I'm the king's law, understand?* And you can take that whether you like it or not."

The punch to his stomach knocked Robin's wind out, but he was not ready to pull his dirk on the bully yet. He swallowed some air and shook his head. Perhaps the lawman would get sick of his badgering, go away, and take his noisome companions with him.

"He don't hear so good," one of the others chimed in. "I have something here that'll prick up his hearing."

He approached Robin with his knife drawn. He lifted the side of Robin's hat brim and pricked his ear just enough to draw blood.

Robin grabbed his staff with both hands to knock his assailant to the ground and then give the other two the beating of their lives. But his action was stopped by the sweetest sound he could imagine. A damsel's voice. A familiar voice. He froze before he could thwack the scoundrel who had cut his ear.

"Stop it!" the lass screamed. "Stop that this moment, you bullies. You are a disgrace. If you lay another hand on that poor old man I will report you to the sheriff."

Her plea unleashed a torrent of merriment from the constables.

"Report us to the sheriff? The sheriff would only be angry that he wasn't here to join in the fun," a constable guffawed.

But the lady's intercession *did* cause a halt to their assault and the three drunken constables went on their way staggering down the street and repeating, "Report us to the sheriff! Ha, ha!"

At length the three scoundrels turned a corner and were out of sight.

Robin was enraptured. He had found his Maid Marian. Or, rather, she had found him. Which was even better.

He did not reveal yet who he was.

"Thank you so much, young lady," he quavered. "If you hadn't come along, there is no telling what would have happened to me." He thought to himself, "Or what would have happened to those blackguards."

"Poor fellow," Marian commiserated. "Is there anything I can do to help you?"

"I am dreadfully thirsty, fair lady," Robin pleaded. "Could you lead me somewhere to get a sip of water for my parched throat?"

"I can do much more than that for you, poor fellow," Maid Marian replied. "I will take you to my cottage for a drink of good brown ale. But first, I must bandage that ear of yours."

Robin knew the knife prick was not deep. But Maid Marian was a very compassionate lass and was determined to give as much succor as possible to the mistreated old blind man.

She took his hand (O bliss!) and led him to her home, which was several lanes away.

"Now let's attend to that ear first," Marian said, as she seated him at her kitchen table.

"If it's all the same to you, Miss," Robin replied. "I would appreciate that mug of ale first. I have a mighty thirst."

Robin wanted to prolong the masquerade a bit longer, enjoying the attention he was receiving from his lady love.

"Of course, you poor thing," Marian commiserated. "The ear can wait."

She opened the larder and brought out a pitcher of good Nottingham ale. She poured Robin a mug.

"Won't you join me?" that rascally Robin asked in the pleading tone of an elderly man.

"If you would like," Marian responded.

Marian poured herself a mug and sat down across the table from the disguised Robin.

Robin was absolutely delighted. As he sipped from his mug he doted on watching Marian's cherry lips descend on the edge of her mug as she drank the sweet frothy brew. His eyes drank in the glory of her voluptuous breasts. And his hands yearned to make a pilgrimage up her thighs to caress her waiting pussy. He could barely control his enthusiasm. But the wily lad made sure it did not show.

He prolonged the experience by sipping slowly while maintaining eye contact between glances at his hostess' boobs.

A strong suspicion crossed Maid Marian's mind. The blind beggar had lively eyes that locked on hers and then peregrinated lasciviously over her body.

"You neglected to remove your hat," she challenged. "In Nottingham Town it is customary for a good yeoman to remove his hat in the house."

Robin chuckled as he took off the floppy-brimmed hat.

"And," continued the lass, "It would be even more polite if you were to remove that false white beard."

Now Robin joined his laughter to hers.

"Robin!" Maid Marian exclaimed. "You zany! I should have recognized you behind that disguise. I knew you would come to me. And here you are."

Robin arose and threw off his tattered coat, revealing himself garbed in his jerkin and tights of Lincoln green.

Maid Marian's eyes gazed at his crotch.

Yes, there was no doubt that outline of the valiant pecker and those proud balls could belong to none other than Robin Hood.

"I was driven mad by your clues," Robin declared. "'At the end of the lane., 'Your enemy's shadow.' But my love for you made me quick witted. And here I am, re-united with the love of my life."

Maid Marian arose and threw her arms around her Robin.

"My clever, clever Robin. Welcome," she laughed.

They united in a close hug. Following the hug, Marian turned her attention to the wound on Robin's ear.

"It's all healed," Marian said.

"What's all healed?"

"The prick on your ear."

"Forget the ear, but not the prick," quoth Robin. "I have waited far too long to taste again those cherry lips and offer my prick for your delectation."

Maid Marian's lips met his, and Robin's very soul melted into that kiss. For Robin, the kiss elicited not only a confirmation of his love, but a re-blooming of his lust.

"Let's get undressed and celebrate our reunion," Robin suggested, with perhaps undue precipitation.

"No," answered his lover. "That cannot be. Not yet."

"And why not, my dear?"

"That is not the way it is done, nowadays," Marian informed him. "After all, it is 1186. These are modern times, Robin, not the Dark Ages."

Robin failed to catch the drift of Maid Marian's talk. 1186? Of course it was. Modern times? What else? What did that have to do with keeping their clothes on when he had looked forward to uniting with his love in the way of man and woman?

"This is the Age of Chivalry," Marian continued. "In order to win a damsel's favor, a man must go forth and prove his love."

"What was that all about?" Robin wondered. Hadn't he already proved his love by finding her?

"Back in May, when you breathed on my cock and ran your dainty fingers over it, weren't you being thoroughly modern?" Robin asked.

"Of course," the lass replied, illogically to Robin's mind. "Maying is one thing. That was a lark. And I thoroughly enjoyed tasting your sweet mouth. And I have looked forward to consummating our love in the way of man and woman ever since. But this is not May. And I am not gathering flowers in the forest. I will gladly take you to my bed, Robin. And we shall have all manner of sport. Whatever it is you have in mind. But first, you must provide me a favor that I ask of you."

"Very well," Robin agreed, his disappointment poorly hidden. "What favor can I regale you with?"

"A gold and silver arrow," the damsel answered. "That will prove your bravery and your devotion."

A gold and silver arrow? *The Gold and Silver Arrow?!* Did Maid Marian know what she was asking? Robin was suddenly wishing they were back in the Dark Ages when the satisfaction of the mating urge wasn't so complicated.

But the brazen lad could not shirk the risk or cower from the danger. For his love he would somehow enter the contest, win the arrow, avoid capture, and return to her and bed her. He would not and could not gainsay that.

"Very well, My Love," he promised. "I shall enter the lists, out-shoot the finest archers in the kingdom, and bring you back the Gold and Silver Arrow you request.

"But for now. What are we going to do to comfort the boner that your presence has aroused?"

Maid Marian was a reasonable lass. And she did insist on being modern and on respecting the chivalric rules.

But she did truly wish to fondle and taste that glorious prick she had breathed on and felt within those tights on May Day.

"You may take off your garb, Robin. But, as a modern damsel, I shall remain clothed in your presence until you bring me the gold and silver arrow.

"I will fondle your love wand until I squirt the nectar out of it.

"When you have recovered from that, I will taste that virile organ and ingest the seed that will regale my mouth.

"But we shall not become more intimate than that until, like the heroes of chivalry, you fetch me the arrow."

Well, it wasn't the fucking he was looking forward to. But getting jacked off and then sucked off the same afternoon wasn't to be sneezed at either.

He disrobed before the love of his life could change her mind.

As it turned out, she gave him as good a hand job as Bess and she was even more talented a cocksucker than Dorothy.

And he knew she would be a terrific fuck once he brought her the God damned arrow.

After having brought him to two exhilarating climaxes, she suggested he put his disguise back on, and return to her when he had complied with the laws of Chivalry.

Robin would not re-don his disguise. He had found his love. The bravest thing to do was to go out into Nottingham Town dressed in his Lincoln green garb, and, with his blackthorn and his dirk, bravely challenge anyone who might dare accost him.

No one in Nottingham challenged the outlaw leader on his departure from the town.

He was a merry Robin. He had found his Maid Marian who had literally found him to her taste.

Lythe and listen, gentilmen,
And herken what I shal say,
How the proud sheryfe of Notyngham
Dyde crye a full fayre play;

That all the best archeres of the north
Sholde come upon a day,
And he that shoteth allther best
That game shall bere away.

He that shoteth allther best,
Furthest fayre and lowe,
At a payre of fynly buttes,
Under the grene wode shawe,

A ryght good arowe he shal have,
The shaft of sylver white,
The hede and feders of ryche rede golde,
In Englond is none lyke.

This than herde good Robyn,
Under his trystell-tre:
'Make you redy, ye wyght yong men:
'That shotynge wyll I se.

'Buske you, my mery yonge men;
Ye shal go with me;
And I wyll wete the sheryfes fayth,
Trewe and yf he be.'

Whan they had theyr bowes i-bent,
Theyr takles fedred fre,
Seven score of wyght young men
Stode by Robyns kne.

Whan they cam to Notyngham,
The buttes were fayre and longe;
Many was the bolde archere
That shot with bowes stronge.

"There shall but syx shote with me.
The other shal kepe my hede,
And stand with gode bowes bent,

That I be not desceyved."

The fourth outlawe his bowe gan bende,
And that was Robyn Hode.
And that behelde the proud sheryfe,
All by the but he stode.

Thryës Robyn shot about,
And always he slist the wand.
And so dyde gode Gylberte
With the whyte honde.

Lytell Johann and gode Scatheloke
Were archeres gode and fre.
Lytell Much and gode Reynolde
The worste wolde they not be.

Whan they had shot aboute,
These archeres fayre and gode,
Evermore was the best,
For soth, Robyn Hode.

Hym was delivered the good arowe,
For best worthy was he.
He toke the yeft so curteysly
To grene-wode wolde he.

A Gest of Robyn Hode
The Fyfth Fytte
Circa 1300 A.D.

CHAPTER SIX

An Arrow for Maid Marian

When Robin returned to his men under the Trystell-tree he informed them of his change of mind.

"Good yeomen," he announced. "While scouting out the gossip in Nottingham Town today, I heard some say that Robin Hood was a coward, fearful of entering the Saint Willibald's Day bowmanship contest."

Cries of "No," "Never," "Liars," erupted from the band.

"I have never heard the word coward applied to me without giving the only response possible. That is, blow the word right back into the face of anyone who dares say it. Coward am I not. Nor can the word be justly applied to any one of you brave yeomen of the forest."

"Hear, hear," resounded throughout the forest from the cheers of the Merrymen.

"I propose," Robin continued, "that sevenscore of us drift into Nottingham Town come Saint Willibald's Day. Some dressed as peasants, some as tinkers, some as beggars, some even as friars. Let each of us don the disguise of his choice. All shall witness the contest of the greatest bowmen in the kingdom and beyond. Let no man remain behind because of fear."

The cheering was even more boisterous than before.

"Sevenscore of us?" asked Littlejohn. "But we are sevenscore and two."

"Sevenscore, I say," Robin repeated. "Two must remain behind to guard our camp. They will be the most valorous of all. Two against any invaders who may take the occasion to enter the forest and do mischief to our home and sanctuary while we are away. For this worthy duty I nominate Allan a Dale and Pym. Allan because the sheriff dealt with him face-to-face and has promised to hang him high. He is too well known by the sheriff and his constables in Nottingham Town to pass through unnoticed. The other one to remain behind shall be Pym. For of us all, he best can make himself invisible in the forest and no one else is as intimately acquainted with the whereabouts of our treasures and provisions."

All agreed that the plan was well thought out.

"Friar Tuck need not disguise himself," Robin continued. "A more innocent looking friar never trod the lanes of the shire."

The men knew that to be the truth. Most doubted that the innocence was aught but a disguise itself.

"Not a one of us shall enter Nottingham Town unarmed," Robin proclaimed. "Each must bring bow or broadsword cleverly hidden from sight. And, of course, let no man venture into the town without his trusty dirk. Save our friar, of course. Let his holy vows make that determination for him. But for the rest of us, there's treachery aplenty in the sheriff's bailiwick and every man jack of us must be prepared to protect his own skin and that of his brothers. For, men, we are brothers all, are we not?"

The response was a deafening assent.

Robin chose six of his men to enter the contest with him. The six were Littlejohn, Will Scarlet, Little Much, Reynold Greenleaf, George a Green and Gandeleyn. The latter two were not to actually participate but to keep their bows bent and in readiness in case any of the outlaws fell in harm's way.

Excitement was high. Here was adventure. Here was defiance. And, of course, here was the chance to see at first hand the greatest master archers in King Henry's and Queen Eleanor's domains in England and on the Continent. For surely there would not only be good Saxon yeomen among the contestants but archers from the king and queen's dominions across the Channel in Normandy, Anjou, and the Aquitaine as well.

On Saint Willibald's Day, Nottingham Town was festooned and beribboned. And it flew the standards of the finest bowmen of England, Scotland, Wales, Normandy, Anjou, and the Aquitaine. At the butts, stands were erected for the finer folk: knights and their ladies, squires and their dames, rich burgers and their wives. At the target end of the range, two elaborate thrones upon a dais awaited the sheriff and his dame. Behind the two dignitaries there was standing room for the most obsequious and the most obnoxious of the shire's constabulary.

The range itself was twoscore paces broad. At the far end stood the target. The mark was one score and ten yards away from the butts. Behind the mark was a striped pavilion to shelter the participants. In the pavilion were set out casks of good brown humming ale to quench the thirst of the archers.

On both sides of the range there were long benches for those burgers who were merchants, shopkeepers, artisans, and landlords. Behind the benches a fence had been placed to shield the gentry from the intrusion of field hands, laborers, land tenants, and other folk of less than affluent means.

People not only from the shire, but from the far reaches of the kingdom gathered that day. Vendors hawking ale, beer, wine, sweetmeats, scones, and fruit circulated through the mobs from early morning and through the length of the match. Bookmakers accepting wagers on the participants were kept busy, and each of them was attended by a burly money taker.

Whores from three shires mixed meretriciously through the crowd. They were subjected to naughty pinches by the more roguish of the males in attendance.

The local hostelries close by the range provided rooms to which the whores hauled their customers from the sporting crowd. The ladies charged a fee of an angel for a full service, less for handjobs and blowjobs.

Many a whore ended the day a wealthy woman.

Excitement was high at the prick of noon when the herald stepped outside a pavilion and sounded a flourish on his long horn. The crowd fell silent to hear the proclamation.

"By the grace of the High Sheriff of Nottingham, on this Day of Saint Willibald[5], in the Year of Our Lord eleven hundred eighty-six, I announce the commencement of a grand festival of bowmanship. A prize of a valuable arrow of pure beaten gold and silver will be presented to the archer who demonstrates the greatest prowess with the longbow.

"In the first round each man shall take his place at the mark in turn and shall shoot at the target. The thirty-two participants who have entered shall each shoot one arrow. The ten archers with the truest arrows will compete in the second round. The three men who prove truest to the target's clout shall then compete with each other to win the Gold and Silver Arrow by elimination.

"Each of the final contestants shall be allowed three shots at the target.

"May the best man win. God save King Henry, Queen Eleanor, the Royal Princes and the realm they rule by Divine Grace."

The herald retired into the pavilion as the wild crowd cheered, some for particular champions, but most just from sheer spiritedness.

After the first qualifying shot, Littlejohn, Will Scarlet, Much the Miller's son, and Reynold Greenleaf were eliminated. They kept their bows bent along with George a Green and Gandeleyn to protect Robin.

The ten archers whose arrows measured within the clout and closest to the center were declared as qualified for the second round. These then paraded from the mark to the butts and back again, some waving to the cheering crowd, some maintaining an aloofness borne of self-satisfaction.

Of the ten, the best known were Gilbert o' the Red Cap, Diccon

---

5   The fabled Nottingham Shooting Match was held on July 9, 1186.

Cruikshank and Adam o' the Dell. These three were cheered the loudest because higher wagers rode on their abilities than on those of the other seven. Swithin o' Hertford, Hubert o' Cloud and William o' Leslie were recognized by the more knowing members of the crowd and received a share of the applause. Three of the contenders had come to England from across the Channel. Pierre Plantagenet was a distant cousin of King Henry and was cheered by the Norman knights and ladies in attendance. Thierry Goncourt from the Aquitaine and Jacques Crevecoeur from Normandy completed the list of the archers from abroad.

There was a tenth contender who drew mainly scoffs from the stands and benches. However, he was an instant favorite of the throngs of rabble behind the fence. This tenth archer was attired in a tattered scarlet robe mended with motley patches. His Lincoln green tights covering a distinctive bulge were the only feature that might have given a clue to anyone. But only a few of the more perceptive ladies noticed.

The stranger wore a patch over his left eye, had a brown bushy beard, and his scraggly hair hung haphazardly down from his wide-brimmed hat.

The sheriff was very interested in the ten contenders. He asked his most trusted constables if they recognized any of them as Robin Hood. The tattered stranger was out of the question. Robin was known to have reddish blond hair and beard and was certainly not partially blind. The others were too famed to be taken for anyone other than who they claimed to be.

"Hell and damnation!" the sheriff declared.

The scoundrel *was* too much of a coward to compete. The trap had failed and a new plan for capturing him would have to be devised.

The ten contenders were allowed to shoot three arrows each. Of these, the three who shot best were Gilbert o' the Red Cap, Adam o' the Dell, and the tattered stranger in scarlet.

The bookmakers were now kept very busy in the new round of betting. Pounds were wagered by those in the stands. Angels were wagered by those on the benches. Pennies were bet by those behind the fence. The stranger in scarlet was the favorite of the penny crowd. He was totally shunned by the bettors in the stands and on the benches.

The sheriff bet heavily on Gilbert. If the king's cousin had made the cut the sheriff would have made a great show of laying his pounds on him to possibly curry favor in London Town. But with Pierre Plantagenet out of the running, the surest bet seemed to be on Gilbert, who was known to be favored by Queen Eleanor if Thierry Goncourt did not survive the preliminaries.

The first archer of the three to toe the mark was Gilbert o' the Red Cap. His arrow struck the clout a finger's width from the center. It was a fine shot and the sheriff was pleased. The tattered stranger was next. There was much laughter on the part of the more privileged classes as they saw him take aim with his one good eye. His arrow was just a mite closer to the center than Gilbert's. The approbation of the mob behind the fence was loud. Adam o' the Dell was next to toe the mark. He shot his arrow which landed right next to the stranger's. A tie. Gilbert o' the Red Cap was eliminated.

The final two contestants were Adam o' the Dell and the scarlet clad stranger.

In the final round, Adam shot first. His three arrows hit just a hairsbreadth from the center of the clout. Wild applause broke out from those in the stands and on the benches.

The stranger shot. His arrows hit the exact center of the target. Adam o' the Dell clapped the stranger on the shoulder.

"Best fucking shooting I've ever seen. Congratulations. You are a credit to all the yeomen in the country, whoever you are."

Pounds had been lost in wagers by the spectators in the stands. Angels had been lost by those on the benches. But many a penny was won by the people who had been confined behind the fence.

The stranger leaned on his bow and smiled at those who had supported him.

The constables had a difficult time controlling the crowd. Everyone seemed to want to descend onto the shooting range. But, the line was held by the constabulary so the presentation ceremony would not be disrupted.

The sheriff descended from the dais clad in his elaborate silks and velvets. His style was very much in the Norman mode. He carried the gold and silver arrow extended before him so it could be seen by all. He stood before the raggedly clad winner of the match.

"Excellent shooting, Fellow," the sheriff pronounced. "You have fairly won the match, and I congratulate you. What is your name, and whence came you?"

"They call me Jock o' Teviotdale, Your Honor," the winner said.

The sheriff presented the gold and silver arrow to the stranger. The crowd from behind the fence set up an enormous cheer.

"Well, Jock o' Teviotdale," the sheriff continued. "I can use a man like you in my service. I will clothe you much in much better attire than those Teviotdale rags you are wearing. I will provide you with the best vittles and drink our England has to offer. Your wage will be fourscore marks. I see that you are a better shot than that knave Robin Hood who was not man enough to show up for the contest. Will you join my service?"

The stranger paused and seemed to give the matter some consideration.

"I must give the matter some thought," he said in a northern accent. "I am a very independent kind of body, as are all our people up Teviotdale way. I am, though, very honored by your offer and promise I will return my answer this evening."

"That is fair enough," said the sheriff. "I know it will be a great change for you to make. So think it over well, and I'm quite sure that you will see that your lot will improve much more here in Nottingham than in Teviotdale."

The constables were not able to hold back the crowd any longer. The spectators surged onto the field. The six Merrymen who were among the contestants closed in on Robin to protect him. The Merrymen in the stands surged onto the field and joined the other outlaws. The sheriff rapidly removed himself from the vulgar crowd and returned to the dais to join his dame.

In the melee of the crowd, Robin removed his tattered coat, his eyepatch, his wide-brimmed hat with the false hair attached, and his false beard and slipped them all to Reynold. Robin was now garbed in his Lincoln green jerkin and tights and slipped away from the crowd, making his way to the home of his own true love bearing the gold and silver arrow that proved his bravery and his devotion to his lady.

When Robin arrived at Maid Marian's home and knocked on the door there was no response. He circled the dwelling, checked doors and looked in windows. It was quite clear that no one was home.

There was nothing to do but wait to see what would happen.

It was a half an hour before he spied Maid Marian scurrying down the lane.

"I'm sorry to have kept you waiting, Robin," she apologized. "I was at the tournament and was delayed in my return by the bustling crowds and by exchanging gossip with my friends Bess and Dorothy. They were with me through the whole match. Come in, come in."

Robin and Maid Marian entered the cottage, closed the door, and engaged in a long, deep, lingering kiss.

They were pressed belly to belly for the kiss. Robin sprang an urgent hardon. But for his disguise, he had oriented his dong in a downward direction and its exertion against his tights was distressing him mightily.

Maid Marian was aware of his problem and reached down into his tights to re-orient the surging organ.

Robin winked at her and thanked her graciously.

When Robin's equipment was facing north, Maid Marian was blushing with excitement.

"Oh, Robin," she exclaimed. "I thought it was you at the contest as soon as I saw you in that ridiculous scarlet coat and that black eyepatch. But when I saw that lovely bulge in your tights, there was no question. I was so proud of you."

"I did it all for love of you, fair damsel," Robin replied in what he hoped was a sufficiently modern, chivalrous manner. "And here, beneath my jerkin, I carry the gold and silver arrow you requested as testimony to the trueness of my devotion."

Robin removed his jerkin, revealing his broad, bare chest. He extracted the arrow hidden in his jerkin, went down on one knee, extended the arrow to Maid Marian, and as she accepted, he blew her a kiss.

"Robin," she said. "You won my heart in May. I have held you therein now for two full months. All that I am now is yours. The gold and silver arrow shall grace yon wall as a constant remembrance of you. But the arrow I treasure most is the one shot into my heart by Dan Cupid. And that arrow bears your own dear name. I treasure that shaft beyond gold, silver, rubies, or diamonds."

"That arrow," Robin responded, "I would present to you in the bedroom. For Dan Cupid has drawn his bow on me, with wicked aim. And my love arrow that you just re-arranged for me, seeks the target you promised it upon presentation of yonder gold and silver one."

Robin thought that was a rather pretty speech. At least it had its desired effect because with the trophy arrow in one hand Maid Marian extended the other to him. He took her hand, arose, and let her lead him into her boudoir.

Maid Marian kissed the arrow and laid it on her dressing table.

"I promised you my favors, Robin," she cooed, "if you performed the act of valor and won for me the gold and silver arrow."

"And when, Fair Marian, may I expect to receive the prize promised by you?" Robin asked. The lusty timbre in his voice was unmistakable.

Robin did not have to wait long. For Maid Marian was looking forward to presenting the long-awaited reward with as much enthusiasm as Robin had felt when anticipating it.

The couple hastily undressed and tumbled into Marian's bed.

Now that he knew she was a sure thing, Robin could exercise patience.

He had to take pleasure in those voluptuous boobs.

As his sweetheart lay on the bed sighing, he applied his lips to those extended nipples that had popped up perkily to greet him.

As he sucked and suckled, Maid Marian's right hand encircled his balls and gave gentle loving squeezes as she employed her left hand to her cunt and matched the rhythm of one hand to that of the other.

Robin laid a hand on his sweetheart's fluffing hand and employed a finger to her clit as she inserted a moistened finger into her hole.

In like fashion, they beguiled the time until neither could hold back from the act they had been awaiting.

Robin mounted his leman, gently entered her, and gave her the fucking he had been dreaming of ever since her hand had grazed his dick on May Day last.

While Maid Marian and Robin were thus involved, Littlejohn and Will Scarlet were standing in the shadows of the house across the lane from the sheriff's headquarters.

Will was carefully wrapping a note around an arrow.

Inside the station the sheriff and fourscore of his constables, deputies, and toadies were feasting and drinking. The sheriff was bragging that Jock o' Teviotdale would soon be joining the force.

"He is unquestionably the finest bowman in the kingdom...and beyond, by God! We need a man who can outshoot that coward Robin Hood who declined to demonstrate his archery skills here today. Jock has been thinking over my offer all afternoon and he will surely accept it. I am a great judge of character. And Jock o' Teviotdale is possibly the canniest man I have ever met. He cannot possibly refuse such an offer."

The pronouncement was met by raucous approval. This was good news indeed. An occasion for tapping the kegs of ale with even more gusto than usual. It would have been very unfortunate if there had been a disturbance anywhere in the shire that evening, for the entire constabulary got very, very drunk.

Across the street, Will was finally satisfied that the note was wrapped about the shaft tightly enough for the arrow's flight to be sure and true.

"Here, Littlejohn," he said. "Inspect the arrow yourself. We would not want it to fly amiss. His Honor the Sheriff is doubtless on pins and needles to hear from his favorite marksman, Jock. We must not keep him waiting too much longer."

Littlejohn inspected the arrow very carefully. He would have to make allowance for the added weight and resistance of the square of parchment. When he was satisfied that he could discharge the missile true, he attached the bowstring to his longbow, nocked the arrow, drew the string to his cheek, sighted on the open window of the building opposite, and let fly.

Satisfied that the mission had been successful, Will Scarlet and Littlejohn disappeared into the Nottingham night.

Inside the station there was widespread consternation. An arrow had flown through an open window and had lodged itself in the side wall. The arrival of the arrow caused an instant halt to the general hilarity.

"Bring me the fucking arrow, Rupert," the sheriff ordered his chief adulator. "It might just be that canny yeoman from Teviotdale's way of informing me that he is about to enter the door and join our throng. It would be just like him. We can use a witty one like him on the force."

Rupert had a bit of difficulty extricating the arrow from its purchase in the wood, but at length he had it whole in his hands. He presented it to his master.

"There appears to be a parchment wrapped around the shaft, Sir," he told the sheriff, handing it over to him.

Since there was writing on the parchment, the sheriff needed someone to read it for him.

"You don't expect me to read this in this light!" the sheriff grumbled. "Read it out loud to me, you fool."

"I was never taught my letters," Rupert apologized.

"Then you, Scribe," the sheriff ordered. "Get up here and read Jock's acceptance of my offer aloud for all of us to relish."

The department scribe hastened to the head table, held the parchment at arms length, and in stentorian voice read the message, which was written in verse.

"The man who won the prize today,
He was not Jock. Oh, nay!
I swear to all, by Holy Rood
He was disguisèd Robin Hood.

The sheriff gave the scribe a sound thwack to the head which sent him reeling onto the ground with a loud thump. The others present did not know whether to laugh or cry at the comic fall of the fat scribe. So everyone simply inserted his nose into his pot and drank deeply.

The sheriff got roaring drunk that night.

Stout Robin Hood, a most lusty out-law,
As ever yet lived in this land,
As ever yet lived in this land.
His equal I'm sure you never yet saw,
So valiant was he of his hand,
So valiant was he of his hand.
No archers could ever compare with these three,
Although from us they are gone;
The like was never, nor never will be,
To Robin Hood, Scarlet and John.
Many stout robberies by these men were done,
Within this our kingdom so wide;
Vpon the highway much treasure they have won,
No one that his purse ere deny'd.
The queen then thought to have her will.

. . . .

Her[Queen Eleanor] little foot-page she sent with all speed,
To find out stout Robin Hood,
Who in the North bravely did live, as we read,
With his bow-men in the green wood.
When as this young page unto the North came,
He staid under a hill at his inn;
Within the fair town of sweet Nottingham,
He there to enquire did begin.
The page then having enquired aright
The way unto Robin Hoods place,
As soon as the page had obtained of him sight,
He told him strange news from her Grace.
'Her Majestie praies you to haste to the court,'
And therewithall shewd him her ring;
We must not delay his swift haste to this sport,
Which then was proclaimd by the king.
Then Robin Hood hies him with all speed he may,
With his fair men attired in green,
And towards fair London he then takes his way;
His safety lay all on the queen.
Now Robin Hood welcome was then to the court,
Queen Katharine [Eleanor] so did allow;
Now listen, my friends, and my song shal report
How the queen performed her vow.
Francis James Child, *The English and Scottish Popular Ballads, Volume III,* #145, Robin and Queen Katherine.

CHAPTER SEVEN

Robin and the Queen

It was Maytime again in Sherwood Forest. One year had passed since the Nottingham archery contest. Maid Marian and her merry friends came into the forest to collect their posies, but no romantic adventures awaited them this Year of Grace 1187. Robin had paid regular visits in scores of disguises to his sweetheart's cottage in Nottingham Town. And much jolly sport ensued within those walls. But in the confines of the greenwood Robin kept himself chaste...except on the rare occasion when a curious nymph sought him out in the depths of his forest haunts.

Towards the end of May, on one of the warm days heralding the advent of summer, Friar Tuck and David of Doncaster sallied out of the forest to the tables of the Blue Boar to refresh themselves with mine host's cool ale. They sat at their favorite table under the spreading oak, contentedly quaffing their pots.

On that lovely day, a small, handsome young man rode up the Lincoln Highway on a milk-white steed. He was as fair as any maiden. His long yellow hair cascaded from under his purple velvet cap onto his shoulders. His winsome cornflower blue eyes sparkled as he recognized the tavern's sign. He was richly attired in silk and velvet. And his embedded jewels flashed in the Maytime sun. At his side he was armed with a jeweled dagger on a jewel-studded sash.

David and Friar Tuck recognized the young man before he dismounted. He was none other than Guillaume de Bois-Guilbert, the page they had previously met right there at the Blue Boar.

Friar Tuck teased his young friend.

"David," he said. "I hope you have brought along a spare pair of tights."

"Why say you that?" David replied.

"When last we sat here with the fair youth who approaches, you and he engaged in a game of lap-hand that left each of your laps wet. And I deem the liquid was not mine host's ale."

David blushed. But did not deign to reply to the jest.

David and Friar Tuck greeted the fair page and led him to their table.

Maken came directly to the table. David ordered a glass of Rhenish wine for the new arrival and asked her to bring a large refill pitcher as well.

The three men drank to each other's health.

"Welcome back to our Nottinghamshire tavern," David said. "Do you return for pleasure or does some special charge bring you to us?"

Guillaume wiped a drop of wine from his lips.

"I am sent, my friends, from London Town by Good Queen Eleanor. I am free now to tell you I am one of her most trusted pages. She has commissioned me to come to the shire to bring a message to the famous outlaw of Sherwood Forest, Robin Hood. I made straight for the Blue Boar in hopes of finding you two, thinking you might be able to assist me in my quest."

"I can arrange a meeting between you and Master Robin," Friar Tuck told Guillaume. "But if your mission could in any way bring harm to him, my holy orders would prevent me from offering such assistance."

"The queen's message is one of peace, not mischief to Master Robin," Guillaume responded. "She proposes an adventure which may interest the leader of the far-famed Merrymen."

"If that be the case," David of Doncaster assured the Norman page, "we can and will take you to Robin's presence."

Before leaving the Blue Boar, David and the friar stood Guillaume to another round of Rhenish and would not allow him to pay. Then, taking a pitcher of wine with them, they entered the greenwood with Guillaume leading his horse by its reins.

As the threesome approached Robin's refuge the sound of raucous music and laughter reached them. They came to the trystell-tree under which the Merrymen were assembled. The outlaws were stretched out under the Great Oak drinking from their horns. Allan a Dale was strumming his harp and singing a ribald song to them. The ballad dealt with "A Lass from Scrooby." Each verse of the song dealt with some humorous escapade of the maid and caused laughter to erupt from Allan's audience. The sight of Friar Tuck and David of Doncaster entering their midst accompanied by an elaborately dressed youth leading a white horse did not disrupt the mirth. It merely added to it. Guillaume tethered his horse at the perimeter of the crowd and, like David and Friar Tuck, sat down on a log to listen to the rest of the song.

When Allan completed his performance to wild acclaim Guillaume was brought to Robin and introduced.

"But we need no introduction," Robin said with a friendly smile. "I remember you well, Guillaume. We previously met at the Blue Boar. Welcome to Sherwood Forest."

Guillaume was amazed that he had actually met the famous Robin Hood the last time he was in Nottinghamshire. He had no idea at the time with whom he was drinking. And he now realized that the singer he had just been listening to was the tinker who had been entertaining the guests at the tavern that last time he was in the shire. He guessed he would have to become accustomed to the fact that he had been among outlaws previously.

Surprised as he was by all this, Guillaume did not forget why he was there.

"Master Robin," he said. "I bring greetings to you from our noble Queen Eleanor. She has heard so much about your brave deeds and fair face that she would be pleased to have you as her guest in London Town. She has commissioned me to inform you that His Majesty King Henry the Second has sponsored an archery tournament at Finsbury Field, to be held next week. Our queen has heard how you won the tournament in Nottingham Town and did so in the presence of the sheriff who seeks your arrest. Her Majesty is not overly fond of the Sheriff of Nottingham and is pleased by your exploit.

"She bade me inform you that if you will come to London Town and engage in the competition at Finsbury Field she can assure you safe conduct. As a sign of her goodwill she removed this gold ring from her thumb and told me to offer it to you."

Robin accepted the ring, kissed it, and slipped it onto his little finger.

Robin told Guillaume, "I am completely at good Queen Eleanor's service and disposition. I am honored and look forward to matching our Midcountry archery skills against the brave men the court may assemble. I will depart at dawn tomorrow. I will bring Littlejohn and Will Scarlet to compete with me. Allan a Dale shall come also to entertain the queen with his minstrelsy. Are you in accord, Sieur Guillaume?"

Guillaume agreed. And he declared that setting out at dawn would be quite satisfactory to him.

"Until then, Guillaume, I hope you will enjoy the rough hospitality we have to offer here in the wilds," Robin invited. "With meat, music and good fellowship we can entertain you abundantly. I am afraid, though, that to quench your thirst we have only ale and the waters of Clough Creek. We are not accustomed to entertain Norman drinkers of wine."

David of Doncaster was at hand to correct Robin.

"Friar Tuck and I took the occasion of our Norman friend's arrival to order a pitcher of good Rhenish wine from Maken. It rests yonder in the shade."

Guillaume spent his afternoon and evening in the forest. The music was merry, the fellowship was jolly, the feasting was plentiful, and David and

Friar Tuck kept him in constant supply of sweet wine.

And although he was well entertained by his hosts. Guillaume de Bois-Guilbert found the Saxon revelries a bit coarse for his Norman taste.

However, he did not turn down the opportunity to bed down with David of Doncaster for the night.

All night long the young fellows taught each other corresponding words in French and English. David learned the Norman-French word for *prick*. Guillaume learned the English word for arse, *cul*. Somehow, much of the night was spent fitting *prick* to *cul*.

Never before did either lad find that learning a new language could be so entertaining.

The travel party was up before dawn the next morning. Robin attired himself in a red jerkin. But he wore his characteristic Lincoln green tights. Allan a Dale wore his blue minstrel garb. Littlejohn and Will Scarlet wore their customary garb. For protection the party wore burnished steel head plates under their caps. Under their jerkins they wore linked mail. After a breakfast of oat cakes and ale the group headed off for London Town, Guillaume taking the lead on his white horse.

It was an uneventful four day journey from Sherwood Forest to the gray walls and towers of London Town. The sight of the four travelers aroused no curiosity on the part of those they encountered on the road.

On the morning of the fifth day Guillaume led his four charges to the Norman palace that housed the royals and their retainers.

Queen Eleanor was in her bower. Her ladies-in-waiting were chatting excitedly as they awaited the arrival of the famous handsome young outlaw.

The queen's chamberlain, Richard Patringten, entered the bower to announce that Guillaume de Bois-Guilbert accompanied by four stout yeomen awaited her pleasure.

"Show them in, Richard," she ordered.

Patringten bowed his way out and returned with Guillaume and the four provincial guests.

The new arrivals approached the queen, dropped to one knee, and doffed their caps.

"I, fair Queen," said the leader of the band, "am Robin Hood, whom you bade come to you.

"I wish to thank you for the gold ring you sent with Guillaume. I wear it on my drawstring hand in honor of Your Majesty.

"I present myself and my boon companions for whatever you would have of us. Myself, Littlejohn, and Will Scarlet offer such poor bowmanship abilities as we may possess. Allan a Dale offers his silver harp and golden tongue to bring you minstrelsy from the mid and north countries, an it please

Your Majesty."

Queen Eleanor was pleased with the appearance of Robin and found his speech agreeable.

She bade him and his companions arise.

When the companions stood up and bowed at Her Majesty and her lovely maids of honor, Queen Eleanor's eyes fairly bugged out when they bored in on the bulge within Robin's tights.

She was not disappointed. Unless the outlaw was wearing falsies, he very much lived up to her expectations.

She told him she had heard of many of his legendary adventures and informed him of the pleasure she derived on hearing how he outwitted that scurvy Sheriff of Nottingham.

But Robin could not help but notice that she directed her speech not to his handsome face but to his awesome crotch.

She told his cock she desired to hear some of its adventures.

Of the further plans she had for it, she revealed not a word.

Eleanor of Aquitaine invited Robin and his companions to join her in the next room to feast while they entertained her and her ladies with tales and song.

The fare in the diningroom involved beef and venison aplenty. There were vegetables that none of the midlanders had ever seen before. But they did manage to eat the foodstuff despite its novelty. There was plenteous Rhenish wine and London beer. However there was no ale. The Midcountry outlaws wisely decided that beer would have to do.

While all ate and drank, Robin regaled the queen and her ladies with one adventure tale after another. Some had already been told by the storytellers and minstrels who had visited the court, because Robin's exploits were well broadcast outside Barnsdale and Sherwood Forest. But the adventures sounded fresh from Robin's lips. The tales dealt not solely with his own adventures. He told amusing stories about Littlejohn and about Will Scarlet. He finished with the tale of how Allan a Dale had disguised himself as a tinker and then fought him and finally ended up as minstrel to the outlaw band. All the ladies seemed to enjoy Robin's stories. But Queen Eleanor laughed the heartiest and toasted each story with a witty remark and a wink at his wonk.

With Allan a Dale's story, it was time for the minstrel to strum his harp and sing to the queen and her ladies.

As Allan sang, Robin was free to let his eye take pleasure in all the damsels present. The queen had surrounded herself with rare beauties. There was no question about that. And, as was his wont, Robin assessed the charms of each one in his mind. But although the queen was much the senior of them all, she had retained the loveliness of youth. Somehow, her face, her figure, her poise, her vivacity, and her earthiness made her an irresistible figure.

As he imagined what a romp with his queen would be like, he was fighting a losing battle with what was going on beneath his tights.

Fortunately, he had previously oriented his dick northward, so at least there was no pain involved as his organ became engorged.

"Your Majesty," Allan suggested. "With the advent of the summer season upon us, perhaps I should begin with the Cuckoo Song."

He strummed the basic tune on his harp, then began:

"Sumer is ycomen in,
Loude sing cuckou!
Grwoeth seed and bloeth meed,
And springth the wode now.
Sing cuckou!

Ewe bleteth after lamb,
Loweth after calve cow,
Bulloc sterteth, bucke verteth,
Merye sing cuckou!
Cuckou, cuckou,
Well singest thou cuckou.
Ne swik thou never now!

"A lively and a timely tune, Fair Minstrel," the queen acclaimed. "Might you follow it up with a drinking anthem?"

A drinking song shall it be, Your Majesty," Allan a Dale complied.

At the queen's words the servants knew exactly what to do and filled the goblets of the ladies and the guests with refreshment. As everyone drank, Allan sang:

"Here I was and here I drank:
Farewel, Dame, and mikle thank.
Here I was and had good cheer,
And here I drank wel good beer."

The queen applauded loudly while the damsels tapped their hands together more daintily.

"Your music raises a lively thirst," Eleanor said. "Now, I would have you regale us with something more ribald."

"I would wager our fair queen would relish the riddling song about the young sister," Littlejohn suggested. "It is a bit naughty, but methinks it would not offend even the most modest of Her Majesty's waiting-women."

The other outlaws agreed with Littlejohn's suggestion.

Allan a Dale strummed out an introduction on his harp. Then his voice rang out:

> *I have a yong suster*
> *For beyond the see.*
> *Manye be the durries*
> *That she sente me.*
> *She sente me the cherye*
> *Withouten any stoon.*
> *And so she dide the dove*
> *Withouten any boon.*
>
> *She sente me the brere*
> *Withouten any rinde.*
> *She bad me love my lemman*
> *Withoute longinge.*
>
> *How sholde any cherye*
> *Be withoute stoon?*
> *And how sholde any dove*
> *Be withoute boon?*
>
> *How sholde any brere*
> *Be withoute rinde?*
> *How sholde I love my lemman*
> *Withoute longinge?*
>
> *When the cherye was a flowr*
> *Thanne hadde it no stoon.*
> *Whan the dove was an ey,*
> *Thanne hadde it no boon.*
>
> *Whan the brere was unbred*
> *Thanne hadde it no rinde.*
> *Whan the maden hath that she loveth*
> *She is withoute longinge.*

All in the audience applauded with enthusiasm. Even those sweet young ladies who did not understand the naughty implications of the riddle.

"With what manner of song may I further regale Her Sweet Majesty?" Allan a Dale asked.

"For your last song, sweet minstrel," Queen Eleanor replied. "I would hear a love song."

"Then, Madame, with all my heart, I will render you a love song that is a great favorite in Nottinghamshire," the singer promised. And he sang:

Bitweene Merch and Averil,
When spray biginneth to spring,
The litel fowl hath hire wil
On hire leod to singe.
Ich libbe in love-longinge
For semlokest of all thinge.
Heo may me blisse bringe.
Ich am in hire baudoun.
An hendy hap ich habbe yhent,
Ichoot from hevene it is me sent.
From alle women my love is lent,
And light on Alisoun.

On hew hire heer is fair ynough.
Hire browe, hire ye blake.
With lossum cheere heo on me laugh.
With middle small and wel ymake.
But heo me wolle to hire take
For to been hire owen make,
Longe to live ichulle forsake,
And feye fallen adown.
And hendy hapich habbe yhent,
Ichoot from hevene it is me sent.
From alle women my love is lent,
And light on Alisoun.

Nightes when I wende and wake,
Forthy mine wonges waxeth wan.
Levedy, al for thine sake
Longinge is ylent me on.
In world nis noon so witer man
That al hire bountee telle can.
Hire swire is whittere than the swan.
And fairest may in town.

And hendy hapich habbe yhent,
Ichoot from hevene it is me sent.
From alle women my love is lent,
And light on Alisoun.

Ich am for wowing al forwake,
Wery so water in wore.
Lest any reve me my make
Ich habbe y-yerned yore.
Bettere is tholien while sore
Than mournen evermore.
Geinest under gore.
And hendy hapich habbe yhent,
Ichoot from hevene it is me sent.
From alle women my love is lent,
And light on Alisoun

When Allan a Dale had completed the lays that delighted Her Majesty, Queen Eleanor dismissed everyone except Robin.

"Thank you, good subjects," she said. "This has been a highly amusing morning thanks to our dear guests. Now I have to discuss the upcoming tournament at Finsbury Fields with the master of Locksley Hall."

Robin was surprised to be referred to by his manorial name. But he immediately recognized that in the eyes of the Norman aristocrats he was seen as a Saxon landholder every bit as much as a poacher in the king's forest.

The queen's ladies and Robin's men quitted the room leaving Eleanor and Robin alone together.

"Are you up to a spot of royal sport this morning, Locksley?" Eleanor of Aquitaine asked the comely outlaw from the midlands with a provocative smile.

Robin had been aware that the attention he had been directing at Eleanor's tits had been reciprocated by similar attention on her part to his crotch. He was not taken totally by surprise at her implied invitation.

"It would be my supreme pleasure to be found capable of any service my queen might have in mind," he answered matching smile to smile.

Eleanor of Aquitaine led the outlaw of Sherwood Forest into a sequestered bower she reserved for special trysts

The queen, Eleanor of Aquitaine, had taken many a lover to her couch. She excelled in the bawdy sport. And she found the outlaw of Sherwood Forest her near equal in innovation and endurance.

For as the lovely queen divested herself of her gowns and petticoats without the need of assistance from her maid, Robin got out of his jerkin and tights in a trice.

As Robin stared, amazed and in awe, at the most beautiful tits in the Western world, Eleanor gazed, awestruck, at the most esthetically gorgeous cock and balls she had ever encountered.

Although he was her subject, Robin took the initiative and bolted directly to that pair of nipples that were winking at him across the room.

Even as he sucked, and clung onto her tits with tenacious suction, the queen directed him to the awaiting bed.

Neither minstrelsy nor history record the intricacies of who did what to whom in what was undoubtedly the greatest fuck-fest of the eleventh century.

So I must leave it to the reader's imagination to determine the scenario that satisfies his or her expectations.

As he relaxed after his private encounter with the queen, Robin hoped he would be able to perform for her equally well with his bow and arrow at Finsbury Field as he just had with his mouth, tongue, hands, fingers, arse, cock and balls.

Let us move on to the next chapter and draw our conclusions about his skill at the butts.

He cloathed his men in Lincoln green,
And himself in scarlet red,
Black hats, white feathers, all alike;
Now bold Robin Hood is rid.
And when he came at Londons court,
Hee fell downe on his knee:
'Thou art welcome, Locksly,' said the queen,
'And all thy good yeomendree.'
The king is into Finsbury field,
Marching in battel ray,
And after follows bold Robin Hood,
And all his yeomen gay.
'Come hither, Tepus,' said the king,
'Bow-bearer after mee,
Come measure mee out with this line
How long our mark shall be.'
'What is the wager?' said the queen,
'That must I now know here:'
'Three hundred tun of Renish wine,
Three hundred tun of beer.

'Three hundred of the fattest harts
That run on Dallom lee;
That's a princely wager,' said the king,
'That needs must I tell thee.'
With that bespake one Clifton then,
Full quickly and full soon;
'Measure no mark for us, most soveraign leige,
Wee'l shoot at sun and moon.'
'Ful fifteen score your mark shall be,
Ful fifteen score shall stand;'
'I'le lay my bow,' said Clifton then,
'I'le cleave the willow wand.'
With that the kings archers led about,
While it was three and none;
With that the ladies began to shout,
Madam, your game is gone!

. . . .

Robin Hood took his bagge from his side,
And threw it down on the green;
William Scadlocke [Scarlet] went smiling away,
'I know who this mony must win.'
With that the queens archers led about,
While it was three and three;
With that the ladies gave a shout,
'Woodcock, beware thyn ee!'
'It is three and three, now,' said the king,
'The next three pays for all;'
Robin Hood went and whispered to the queen,
'The kings part shall be but small.'
Robin Hood he led about,
He shot it under hand,
And Clifton, with a bearing arrow,
He clave the willow wand.
And little Midge, the Miller's son,
Hee shot not much the worse;
He shot within a finger of the prick.

. . . .

'A boon, a boon,' Queen Katherine [Eleanor] cries,
'I crave on my bare knee

That you will angry be with none
That is of my party.'
'They shall have forty days to come,
And forty days to go,
And three times forty to sport and play;
Then welcome friend or fo.'
'Then thou art welcome, Robin Hood,' said the queen,
'And so is Little John,
So is Midge [Much], the Miller's son;
Thrice welcome every one.'
'Is this Robin Hood?' the king now said;
'For it was told to mee
That he was slain in the pallace-gate,
So far in the North Country.'
Most bravely and with great might,
But brave jolly Robin shot under his hand,
And then did hit the mark right.
And Clifton he then, with his arrow so good,
The willow-wood cleaved in two;
The Miller's young son came not short, by the rood,
His skill he most bravely did show.
Thus Robin Hood and his crew won the rich prize,
From all archers that there could be;
Then loudly unto the king Queen Katherine[Eleanor] cries,
Forgive all my company!
The king then did say, that for forty daies,
Free leave then to come or go,
For any man there, though he got the praise,
'Be he friend,' quoth he, 'or be he foe.'
Then quoth the queen, Welcome thou art, Robin Hood,
And welcome, brave bow-men all three;
Then straight quoth the king, I did hear, by the rood,
That slain he was in the countrey.

. . . .

Then Robin Hood pardon had straight of the king,
And so had they every one;
The fame of these days most loudly does ring,
Of Robin Hood, Scarlet and John.

Francis James Child, *The English and Scottish Popular*
Ballads, Volume III, Number 145

CHAPTER EIGHT

The Contest at Finsbury Field

The next morning was tournament day at Finsbury Fields[6]. The event was established in a meadow outside the gray walls of London Town. At one end of the field ten pavilions had been raised, one for each of the ten companies of the king's yeomen. One of the center pavilions flew the yellow flag of Captain Tepus, the king's bow-bearer. Atop the next pavilion flew the blue flag of Gilbert of the White Hand. From atop the pavilion on the other side of Tepus' waved the blood-red pennant of Clifton of Buckinghamshire. Pavilions for other companies flew the flags and pennants of Edgar of Kent and William of Southampton, among others.

A score and ten yards from the mark stood ten targets, one for each team.

On either side of the archery range, stands were erected for the great men and women of the realm. And in the center of the north side of the range, under a shaded dais, stood the two thrones for the king and the queen. The stands were packed with spectators, for this was an event that drew enormous interest.

At the sound of trumpets, King Henry and Queen Eleanor arrived at the field. The king sat astride a dapple-gray stallion. The queen rode a milk-white palfrey. Everyone arose as the royals dismounted and ascended the dais. It was noticed by the subjects that their king appeared pale and in possibly failing health. His queen looked as robust as always.

At a second blast of the trumpets, the competing teams exited their pavilions to a cheering crowd. They marched about the perimeter of the field and came to stand at attention before the king and queen. Simultaneously

---

6   The Royal Tournament at Finsbury Fields was held on June 11, 1187.

every bowman went down on one knee and doffed his hat.

Their majesties bade them arise to listen to Sir Hugh de Mowbray announce the rules of the match.

Sir Hugh mounted the dais, doffed his hat and knelt before the king and queen. He then stood to one side and made his announcement.

In the first round, ten archers from each team would shoot three arrows into that team's target. The judges would inspect the targets and determine which three teams had the most arrows within the clout.

The captains of those three teams would then compete by shooting three arrows each.

The winner of that match would receive a purse of twoscore and ten golden pounds, a silver bugle inlaid with gold, and a quiver with ten white arrows tipped with gold and feathered with white swan feathers. The second best archer would receive a patent allowing him fivescore bucks that roamed on Dallen Lea, to be shot at the yeoman's pleasure. The third prize was two tuns of good Rhenish wine.

All who had competed would receive fourscore silver pennies as recognition for their participation.

After the first round, the final competitors were determined. They were Tepus, Gilbert of the White Hand, and Clifton of Buckinghamshire.

The three captains stepped to the mark, aimed, and shot. All three were close in ability, but Gilbert of the White Hand won first prize, Tepus second, and Clifton of Buckinghamshire third.

Queen Eleanor looked the three men over and scoffed. To her husband she asked contemptuously, "Henry. Do you really believe those three to be the finest bowmen in the land?"

Henry was quite proud of all three.

"I believe them to be not only the three best archers in the land, but in the entire world," the monarch replied.

Eleanor teased him. "What if I could produce three archers who can outshoot them?"

"Impossible," sneered the king. "No three archers can outshoot Tepes, Gilbert and Clifton. We have witnessed their skill here today. They are simply the best."

"I believe I can produce three who can outshoot them," Eleanor bantered back.

"Don't speak nonsense," Henry scoffed.

"Would you care to wager on what you call nonsense, Henry?" Eleanor asked.

King Henry loved to gamble. But wanted to find out more about whom he would be betting against.

"Who are the three men you are proposing?"

"They are from the Midcountry," Eleanor told him. "They have run somewhat afoul of the law. If you will grant them pardon for forty days, I will call them forth."

The king was intrigued. During their entire marriage the royal couple had wagered again and again. Eleanor often surprised Henry with the canniness of her betting. But he had full confidence in the shooting abilities of his men.

"You're on," he said.

"What is the size of your wager, Henry?"

"Ten tuns of Rhenish wine, ten tuns of stoutest ale, and tenscore bows of tempered yew with quivers and arrows to match."

Eleanor thought it over.

She had chosen ten husky Saxons who would be her fuckmates in rotation for the following fortnight. She could gift the young stalwarts with such loot in accordance with each one's performance in bed.

"Agreed," she laughed.

"And what do you propose to match my wager, My Dear?" Henry asked.

"I will put up this girdle I am wearing about my waist. As you can see, it is set with enough precious jewels to match and even exceed your wager."

Henry observed the girdle closely. The Countess of Milan was visiting England at the time. She had managed to withstand the king's advances. Henry had been feeling a bit under the weather recently, but he was quite anxious to enjoy the considerable charms of the countess. With the offer of such a girdle he felt sure he could lure her into his bed. And he knew his health, though waning, was still up to showing the countess a merry old English time.

The royal cock was now less reliable than hitherto. But the countess had cocksucking lips which surely could hoist the flag again on high and lead His Majesty once more to a worthy victory.

"You have yourself a bet," the king said.

"And a promise of safety from the law for my miscreant archers as well?" the queen insisted.

"Of course. Forty days of royal pardon," Henry promised. "When can you produce these so-called provincial prodigies?"

Eleanor summoned her page Guillaume.

"Bring forth the men from the Midcountry," she ordered.

Little Guillaume hurried off and within minutes returned with three of the queen's contenders and their bow-bearer.

Guillaume proceeded to the dais followed by a yeoman clad in red accompanied by two men in Lincoln green. A fourth yeoman, in blue, carrying three bows and three quivers, brought up the rear. All five bent the knee and doffed their caps to the royals.

The queen bade them arise and addressed Robin.

"Locksley, I have a wager with the king that you and two of your men can outshoot any three archers he chooses. Will you and your men do your best to win me my wager?"

Robin responded loud and clear, so everyone in the stands could hear his reply.

"That I swear, Your Majesty," he said with a courtly bow.

Having vowed to serve the queen's pleasure, the Northern outlaws were escorted from the royal presence.

"Who is that Locksley?" the king asked aside.

"He is Robin Hood of Sherwood Forest, Henry."

"You don't mean to tell me you have brought to London Town the fellow who outsmarted that dunce of a Sheriff of Nottingham."

"The very same, Husband."

"My but you are the crafty one, Eleanor," Henry complimented her. "I have sorely wished to see that outlaw shoot. I feel that his reputation outshines his provincial ability. I hope so, anyway, for the sake of our little wager. I am happy to grant him and his companions forty days amnesty from the clutches of our law just for the treat of seeing how good these poachers of my deer can perform on a target. I hear they do well shooting at my deer. But my harts are large and yonder clouts are small and distant."

The queen smiled to herself. She well knew how Robin could shoot with his glorious personal arrow.

King Henry sent a page to summon Gilbert, Tepus, and Clifton.

Queen Eleanor simultaneously sent Guillaume to escort Robin, Littlejohn and Will back into the royal presence.

When the king's archers were assembled before the dais, King Henry addressed them thus:

"Tepus, Gilbert and Clifton. My heart was filled with pride at your performance at the butts this morning. Our gracious queen has brought forth three contenders from the Midcountry whom you see standing here. Queen Eleanor and I have a wager. I swear you can outshoot any archers on earth and I have bet on you. The queen challenges with the good yeomen from Nottinghamshire. If you consent to engage them in an archery contest I will fill your caps with silver pennies if you win. But if you lose, you will lose the prizes you have just won. Will you accept my royal challenge?"

With one voice the three answered, "Right willingly, my liege."

"Then to the butts," King Henry shouted.

"And may the best men win," the queen's voice rang out over the crowds in the stands.

Word spread immediately to the archers in their pavilions and to the people in the stands that Robin Hood, Littlejohn, Will Scarlet, and Allan a Dale were the yeomen who had been presented to the king and queen. Robin's fame had spread throughout the realm through minstrelsy and itinerant story tellers. And people were amazed that he was right there at Finsbury Field with three of his outlaw companions, all quite free. Next, word buzzed throughout the crowd that the king had granted to Robin and to his outlaw companions a forty day amnesty. The crowds were fascinated. Here were four notorious robbers and poachers right in their midst. And they were going to compete in a shooting match with the three newly acclaimed champion archers in the king's service.

Six new butts were set up. The six contestants toed their marks and strung their bows.

Clifton of Buckinghamshire was the first contestant. He toed firmly to the mark, fitted his arrow, breathed on his fingers and drew the string slowly and carefully. His arrow sped true and lodged in the white. He shot again, and again hit the clout. The third arrow missed the white but was a mere finger's width into the black. These were his finest shots of the day.

Will Scarlet was next to draw bow. He was overly-nervous, held the string too long, and hit the red, which was the ring beyond even the black. Robin scolded him for over caution. Will then managed to relax and hit the white eye of the target with his next two shots.

Clifton had outshot Will, which pleased the king. But Eleanor was sure Robin and Littlejohn would do better.

Most of the crowd was rooting for the king's men. But the three Midcountry shooters had their share of spectators sympathetic to them. So although there were no bookmakers in the stands, there was a fair amount of wagering going on among individuals.

This first round sent money from those betting on the provincials to those betting on the establishment.

Tepus shot next. His first shot went into the white. On the second shot he held the string too long and his arrow smote the black. His third arrow, though, hit the very center of the clout. Robin congratulated him on a beautiful shot.

Littlejohn took his place at the mark. His was a very different style of shooting from anything seen before at Finsbury Field. The large man shot his three arrows one right after the other. He never lowered the bow but fitted each arrow with his longbow raised. All three of his arrows hit the white, and well away from the black. Some bettors in the stands had given odds against the midlanders and lost a fair amount of money on Tepus.

The king swore an oath, albeit a good natured one. He was a connoisseur of good archery and admired Littlejohn's unique style.

Gilbert stepped up to the mark next. As in his previous trial, all three of his arrows struck into the clout. Robin congratulated him and told him he should be out in the greenwood, not stuck within London's gray walls.

"Come pay us a visit sometime in Sherwood Forest," Robin invited. "A man like you would love the freedom there. And marksmanship like that is fully appreciated by my Merrymen."

Robin stepped up to the mark. Unlike the silence and concentration shown by previous contenders, he kept up his chatting with Gilbert even as he unloosed his arrows. His nonchalance was observable even from the stands. He shot all three of his arrows in a cluster at the very center of the target so the feathers were all ruffled together. His shots looked like one thick shaft.

Londoners had never seen such shooting before. Nor have they since. The crowd, despite the fact that most favored the king's men, let out a roar of approval.

Even King Henry could not help cheering.

"Eleanor," he laughed. "You've outfoxed me again. Your backwoodsmen were superb. You have won our bet fair and square."

The yeomen of the archer guard crowded around the midland shooters to congratulate them. Then, everyone had to step back so the judges could come forward with the official verdict.

They presented Robin with the purse of twoscore and ten golden pounds, the silver bugle, and the quiver with the ten gold-tipped arrows. To Littlejohn they presented the parchment entitling him to shoot fivescore harts that ran on Dallen Lea. And to Clifton was handed the title to two tuns of good Rhenish wine.

Robin spoke forth in response.

"I will keep the silver bugle in remembrance of this historic shooting match. However, to you, Gilbert, I give this purse of gold as tribute to your skill. The arrows you may distribute among those you deem the finest archers."

Gilbert accepted the prizes graciously.

Littlejohn spoke up next.

"Good friend Tepus. I have no need for license to shoot harts on Dallen Lea. I have more of the king's deer than I know what to do with in Sherwood Forest."

Tepus was aware that there was sense in what Littlejohn had said, and accepted the parchment.

Clifton of Buckinghamshire had won the two tuns of Rhenish wine outright.

That afternoon and evening, Robin and his three companions roamed London Town freely. Those who had been at the shooting match recognized them and would not allow them to spend a penny.

Will, Allan, and Littlejohn were freely entertained at London's finest whorehouses by the capital's most capital harlots.

The sexual gymnastics of the ladies were far beyond anything the good yeomen had encountered in the mid-and north-countries. They knew they would never again find such sexual entertainment again, and cheerfully devoted themselves more to heartily fucking than to drinking until their vaunted stamina ran out.

Robin enjoyed himself well in the city but declined the invitations of the Paphians. He was saving his libidinous reservoir for his date that evening with his queen.

At about sunset, Guillaume de Bois-Guilbert found the four companions at the Pig and Whistle. He informed Robin that the queen desired an audience.

Robin returned to the palace with Guillaume, and was very well entertained by his queen. However, he was able to entertain her in return, since he had learned a great deal from her the previous evening.

Matching his Saxon cock to Eleanor's Aquitainian cunt that evening, the Battle of Hastings was re-enacted with victory achieved by both sides. French savoir-faire united with Saxon bravado. The result was the finest sex the island had known until that enchanted evening.

The next day, the four yeomen returned to Nottinghamshire and the life they relished. They bore the amnesty for themselves and for the entire band with them. Great revelry broke out in Sherwood Forest at the news that the outlaw gang would enjoy full amnesty for forty days.

> *Robyn stode in Bernysdale,*
> *And lenyd hym to a tre.*
> *And bi him stode Lytell Johann*
> *A gode yeman was he.*
>
> *And also dyd gode Scarlok,*
> *And Much, the myller's son.*
> *There was none ynch of his bodi*
> *But it was worth a grome.*
>
> *Than bespake Lytell Johnn*
> *All untoo Robyn Hode.*
> *Maister, and ye wolde dyne betyme*
> *It wolde doo you muche gode.*

Than bespake hym gode Robyn.
To dyne have I noo lust
Till that I have some bolde baron
Or som unketh gest

Tyl that I have som bolde baron
That may pay for the best.
Or some knyght or som squyer
That dwelleth here bi west.

A gode maner than had Robyn,
In londe where that he were.
Every day or he wolde dyne
Thre messis wolde he here.

The one in the worship of the Fader,
And another of the Holy Gost.
The thirde was of Oure dere Lady
That he loved allther moste.

Robyn loved Oure dere Lady,
For dout of dydly synne.
Wolde he never do compani harme
That ani woman was in.

"Maister," than sayde Lytell Johann,
"And we our borde shal sprede,
Tell us wheder that we shal go
And what life that we shal lede.

"Where we shal take, where we shal leve,
Where we shall abide behynde.
Where we shal robbe, where we shal reve.
Where we shal bete and bynde."

"Thereof no force," than sayde Robyn.
We shall doo well inowe.
But loke ye do no husbonde harme
That tylleth with his ploughe.

"Noo more ye shall no gode yeman
That walketh by grene-wode shawe,
Ne noo knyght ne noo squyer

That wolde be a good felawe.

"These bisshoppes and these archebishoppes
Ye shall them bete and bynde.
The hye sheryfe of Notyngham
Hym holde ye in your mynde."

"This worde shalbe holde," sayde Lytell Johann,
And this lesson we shall lere.
It is fer dayes, God sende us a gest
That we were at oure dynere."

"Take thy gode bowe in thy honde," sayde Robyn.
"Late Much wende with the.
And so shal Willyam Scarlok,
And no man abyde with me.

"And walke up to the Saylis
And so to Watlinge Strete.
And wayte after some unkuth gest
Up chaunce ye may theme mete.

"Be he erle, or ani baron,
Abbot, or ani knyght,
Bringhe hym to lodge to me.
His dynere shall be dyght."

They went up to the Saylis,
These yemen all three.
They loked est, they loked weest,
They might no man se.

But as they loked in to Bernysdale,
Bi a dernë street,
Than came a knight ridinghe.
Full sone they gan hym mete.

All dreri was his semblaunce,
And lytell was his pryde.
His one fote in the styrop stode,
That othere wavyd beside.

His hode hanged in his iyn two.

He rode in symple aray.
A soriar man than he was one
Rode never in somer day.

Lytell Johann was full curteyse,
And sett hym on his kne.
"Welcom be ye, gentyll knyght,
Welcom are ye to me.

"Welcom be thou to grenë wode,
Hendë knight and fre.
My maister hath abiden you fastinge,
Syr, al these oures thre."

"Who is thy maister?" sayde the knight.
Johann sayde, "Robyn Hode."
"He is a gode yeman," sayde the knight.
"Of hym I have herde muche gode.

"I graunte," he sayde, "with you to wende,
My bretherne, all in fere
My purpos was to have dyned to day
At Blith or Dancastere."

Furth than went this gentyll knyght,
With a carefull chere.
The teris oute of his iyn ran,
And fell down by his lere.

They brought him to the lodge dore,
Whan Robyn gan hym se.
Full curteysly dyde of his hode
And sett hym on his knee.

"Welcome, sir knyght," than sayde Robyn.
"Welcome art thou to me.
I have abyden you fasting, syr,
All these oures thre."

Than answered the gentyll knyght,
With wordes fayre and fre.
"God the save, gode Robyn,
And all thy fayre meyne."

They wasshed togeder and wiped bothe
And sette to theyr dynere.
Brede and wyne they had right inowe,
And noumbles of the dere.

Swannes and fessauntes they had full gode,
And foules of the ryvere.
There fayled none so lytell a birde
That ever was bred on bryre.

"Do gladly, syr knight," sayde Robyn.
"Gramarcy, syr," sayde he.
"Suche a dynere had I nat
Of all these wekys thre.

'If I come ageyne, Robyn,
Here by thys contrë,
As gode a dynere I shall the make
As thou haest made to me."

"Gramarcy, knight," sayde Robyn.
"My dynere what I have
I was never so gredy, bi dere worthi God,
My dynere for to crave.

"But pay or ye wende," sayde Robyn.
"Me thynketh it is gode ryght.
It was never the maner, by dere worthi God,
A yeman to pay for a knyght."

"I have nought in my cofers," sayde the knyght,
"That I may profer for shame."
"Lytell Johann, go loke," sayde Robyn,
"Ne lat not for no blame.

"Tel me truth," than sayde Robyn,
So God have parte of the."
"I have no more but ten shelynges," sayde the knight,
"So God have parte of me."

"If thou have no mere," sayde Robyn,
"I woll not one peny.
And yf thou have need of any more

More shal I lend the.

"Go nowe furth, Lytell Johann,
The trouth tel thou me.
If there be no mere than ten shelynges,
No peny that I se."

Lyttell Johann sprede downe hys mantel
Full fayre upon the grounde.
And there he fonde in the knyghtes cofer
But even halfe a pounde.

Lytell Johann late it lye full styll
And went to hys maister full lowe.
"What tydyngs, Johann?" sayde Robyn.
"Sir, the knyght is trewe inowe."

"Fyll of the best wyne," sayde Robyn.
"The knyght shall begynne.
Muche wonder thinketh me
Thy clothynge is so thinne.

"Tel me one worde," sayde Robyn.
"And counsel shal it be.
I trowe thou wert made a knyght of force,
Or ellys of yemanry.

"Or ellys thou hast been a sori husbonde,
And lyved in stroke and strife.
An orkerer, or ellis a lechoure," sayde Robyn,
"Wyth wronge hast led thy lyfe."

"I am none of those," sayde the knight,
By God that made me.
An hundred winter here before
Myn auncetres knyghtes have be.

"But oft it hath befal, Robyn,
A man hath be disgrate.
But God that sitteth in heven above
May amende his state.

"Withyn this two yere, Robyn," he sayde,

"My neghbours well it knowe,
Foure hundred pounde of gode money
Ful well than might I spende.

"Now have I no gode," sayde the knight.
"God hath shaped such an ende.
But my chyldren and my wyfe,
Tyl God yt may amende."

"In what maner," than sayde Robyn,
"Hast thou lorne thy rychesse?"
"For my greate foly," he sayde,
"And for my kyndenesse.

"I had a sone, for soth, Robyn,
That sholde have ben myn ayre.
Whan he was twenty winter olde,
In felde wolde iust full fayre.

He slewe a knyght of Lancashire,
And a squyer bolde.
For to save him in his right
My godes beth sette and solde.

"My londes beth sett to wedde, Robyn,
Untyll a certayne day,
To a ryche abbot here beside
Of Seynt Mari Abbey."

"What is the som?" sayde Robyn.
"Trouth than tell thou me."
"Sir," he sayde, "foure hundred pounde,
The abbot told it to me."

"Nowe and thou lese thy londe," sayde Robyn,
"What shall fall of the?"
"Hastely I wol me buske sayde the knight
Over the saltë see,

"And se where Criste was quyke and dede,
On the mount of Calverë
Fare wel, frende, and have gode day.
It may not better be."

Teris fell out of hys iyn two.
He wolde have gone hys way.
"Farewel, frendes, and have gode day,
I ne have noo more to pay."

"Where be thy frendes?" sayde Robyn.
"Syr, never one wol me knowe.
While I was ryche inowe at home
Great boste than wold they blowe.

"And nowe they renne away fro me,
As bestis on a rowe.
They take no more hede of me
Than they me never sawe."

For ruthe than wept Lytell Johann,
Scarlok and Much in fere.
"Fyll of the best wyne," sayde Robyn,
"For here is a simple chere.

"Hast thou any frendes," sayde Robyn,
"Thy borowes that wyll be?"
"I have none," than sayde the knight,
"But God that dyed on tree."

"So away thy japes," sayde Robyn.
"Thereof wol I have none.
Wenest thou I wolde have God to borowe,
Peter, Poule, or Johann?

"Nay, by hym that made me,
And shope both sonne and mone,
Fynde me a better borowe," sayde Robyn,
"Or money getest thou none."

"I have none other," sayde the knight,
"The soothe for to say,
But yf yt be Our dere lady,
She fayled me never or thys day."

"By dere worthy God," sayde Robyn,
"To seche all Englonde thorowe,
Yet fonde I never to my paye

A moche better borowe.

"Come nowe furth, Lytell Johann,
And go to my tresourë,
And bringe me foure hundered pound,
And loke well tolde it be."

Furth than went Lytell Johann,
And Scarlok went before.
He told oute four hundred pounde
By eight and twenty score.

"Is thys well tolde?" sayde lytell Much.
Johann sayde, "What greveth the?
It is almus to helpe a gentyll knyght
That is fal in povertë."

"Maister," than sayde Lytell Johann,
"His clothinge is full thynne.
Ye must gyve the knight a lyveray
To lappe his body therein.

"For ye have scarlet and grene, maister,
And many a riche array.
There is no marchaunt in mery Englond
So ryche, I dare well say."

"Take hym thre yerdes of every colour,
And loke well mete that it be."
Lytell Johann toke none other mesure
But his bowë tree.

And at every handful that he met
He lept over fotes three.
"What devylles drapar," sayd litell Much,
"Thynkest thou for to be?"

Scarlok stode ful stil and loughe,
And sayde, "By God Almyght,
Johnn may gyve hym gode mesure,
For it costeth hym but light."

"Maister," than said Lytell Johann

All unto Robyn Hode.
"Ye must give the knyght a hors
To lede home all this gode."

"Take him a gray courser," sayde Robyn,
"And a saydle newe.
He is Oure Ladye's messangere.
God graunt that he be trewe."

"And a gode palfrey," sayde lytell Much,
"To maytene hym in his right,"
"And a payre of botes," sayde Scarlok,
"For he is a gentyll knyght."

"What shalt thou gyve hym, Lytell Johann?" sayde Robyn.
"Sir, a payre of gilt sporis clene,
To pray for all this company,
God bringe hym oute of tene."

"Whan shal mi day be," said the knight,
"Syr, and your wyll be?"
"This day twelve moneth," sayde Robyn,
"Under this grene-wode tre.

"It were greate shame," sayde Robyn,
"A knight alone to ryde
Withoutë squyre, yeman, or page,
To walkë by his side.

"I shal the lende Lytell Johann, my man,
For he shalbe thy knave.
In a yeman's stede he may the stande,
If thou greate nedë have.

A Gest of Robyn Hode
The First Fytte
Circa 1300 A.D.

CHAPTER NINE

The Impoverished Knight

Before the forty day amnesty period had elapsed, the king who had granted it had died. For good King Henry's health was failing even when Robin and his three companions were at Finsbury Field.

Prince Richard, known as the Lion-Hearted, was in Normandy when his father's death was immanent. Before Henry passed into eternity, Prince Richard and his brother, John Lackland, were with their mother, Eleanor of Aquitaine, at his bedside.

Throughout the realm, the cry went out, "The king is dead. Long live the king."

On July third, in the year eleven eighty-nine, Prince Richard was crowned King Richard I, Coeur de Lion.

When word of the old king's death reached Robin, he grieved. For he was grateful for the amnesty granted him and his men by the monarch. And he knew how Queen Eleanor must mourn.

But, at the same time, he welcomed the arrival of the new sovereign, and was aware that Richard the Lion-Hearted would be a better monarch over the Saxon yeomen of the realm than his sinister brother, John Lackland, could possibly be.

Robin, accompanied by Littlejohn, Will Scarlett, and Much the miller's son, were huddled in the greenwood just beyond the borders of Barnsdale. While Robin was expressing his thoughts about the royal succession, Littlejohn's belly was roiling.

"Master," he interrupted the discourse. "Your observations on the state of the realm are pleasing enough to my ears. But my belly has other matters on its mind. It informs me that the dinner hour has arrived."

Robin did not possess as lusty a belly as his large lieutenant. And, moreover, he was much given to having a guest accompany him at his meals.

"I do not choose to dine, Littlejohn, unaccompanied by a titled guest."

"By which you mean a baron, knight, or squire, I suppose," Littlejohn answered.

"Such is my meaning," quoth Robin.

"Then may God soon send us such a guest," Littlejohn yearned. "Else my belly shall begin to rebel against me mightily."

"God will send us our guest only if you seek," Robin advised him. "Littlejohn, take Much and Will with you into Barnsdale. Proceed on past Sayles and then troll through Wattling Street. Thus seeking, you will surely encounter an earl, baron, abbot, or knight. Invite such a one to dine with us. You know how to be very persuasive, my friend."

The three outlaws sallied into Barnsdale while Robin retired to the lodge that had been built in the greenwood abutting Barnsdale to await the guest he knew would be joining him for dinner.

As Robin had predicted, the three Merrymen encountered a knight riding down Wattling Street. But a knight with an aspect they did not expect.

For such a dreary looking knight was hardly to be found in all England. He had but one foot in a stirrup, his hood covered his eyes, and his clothing was mangy indeed.

While Much and Will stayed somewhat to the side, Littlejohn approached the knight.

"Welcome to the greenwood, gentle knight," he said. "My master has held back taking his dinner for three full hours while awaiting your arrival. He invites you to be his guest."

"And who might this master of yours be?" asked the bedraggled knight.

Littlejohn informed him. "Robin Hood."

"Ah, Robin Hood," the knight replied. "I have heard of him. He is reputed to be a good yeoman. I had planned to dine in Blythe or Doncaster this afternoon. But I would be delighted to break bread with Master Robin Hood instead."

So the three outlaws led the sorry knight to the lodge in the forest.

Robin was right pleased with the guest his men had brought to dinner and greeted him with formal courtesy.

After washing their hands and faces, Robin and his guest sat down to enjoy their dinner. Pym served them a banquet of deer liver, swan, pheasant, fish, bread and wine.

The knight and the outlaw ate heartily. The knight thanked Robin and told him it had been a long time since he had eaten so well.

"If I should come this way again," the knight promised, "you shall be my guest. And I will bring provisions to equal this lovely repast you have served me."

"I am delighted to hear that, Sir Knight," Robin responded. "And I look forward to that day. But, in all humility, I must admit I am not a man of great patience. So I would prefer that you pay now for what you have eaten. For I do not believe it is the custom in the realm for a yeoman to pay for a knight's feast."

"I am ashamed to have to tell you, Robin," the knight answered, "that I am a very impoverished knight. I have little coin and no gold nor silver in my coffers. If I did, I would most willingly give you from my horde to exchange for the plenteous feast with which you have regaled me. All I carry with me, though, alas! is ten shillings."

Robin was not one to take his guests at their word about the contents of their purse. So he warned the knight.

"If it be true, Sir Knight, that you bear no more than ten shillings, I will not relieve you of so much as a penny. And what is more, I will lend money to you to carry you on your way. But if you are not true to your word, I will relieve you of most of what you have."

With that promise, Robin bade Littlejohn empty the knight's purse and coffers to verify his guest's declaration.

Littlejohn went to inspect the knight's belongings. He spread his mantle on the ground and emptied those belongings onto the cloth.

When Littlejohn returned to the table, Robin asked him the tidings.

"Your guest, the knight, speaks true, Robin," John answered. "He bears with him less than half a pound."

Robin was pleased to hear that his guest spoke true. But, at the same time, he felt compassion for the doleful knight.

To Pym he ordered, "Go bring in the best wine in the cave for our pauper knight. Fill our flagons with the best we have."

As they sipped the fine wine, Robin addressed his guest.

"It is now little wonder to me that you are traveling so poorly-clad. From your demeanor I judge that you were once a gentleman of some means. Yet it is apparent that you are close to penniless now. I cannot help but wonder what has happened to your previous means.

"Perhaps you managed your affairs poorly. Or were you perhaps usurious or lecherous and thus squandered all your fortune?"

In response to Robin's conjectures, the knight smiled the sorriest grin that his host had ever witnessed.

"No, Friend Robin," he replied. "It was not like that at all. I am of a titled family whose ancestry reaches back for ages. But, as can befall a man of any background, misfortune overtook me.

"Some two years ago, I was in great need of four hundred pounds.

And, although I had lands and rents enough, I did not have access to such a great sum."

Robin asked how the knight had come to such a pass.

"My son and heir," quoth the knight, "is a sporting lad. And a fabled jouster. In an unfortunate mishap, whilst jousting in Lancashire, he slew a powerfully connected knight. To pay the indemnity for my son's action, I was subject to confiscation of all my holdings and goods.

"The abbot of Saint Mary's Abbey in York, lent me four hundred pounds, accepting all my lands and goods as collateral. I must repay him within this week, or all that I have is forfeit."

"And if you do not discover a way to come into the sum of four hundred pounds, what will become of you?" Robin asked.

"All I can do, in that case, is flee England," the knight explained. "I will head for the Holy Land to seek such fortune as may await me in those far-off reaches. And so, Robin, you know my sad tale. And on that note, I will take my leave of you."

As the doleful knight arose, tears streamed down his cheeks.

"Wait," Robin called out. "Have you no friends who will stand security for the sum?"

"Friends!" scoffed the knight. "When I was rich, before everything I had was confiscated from me, I had friends aplenty. Now, when any of them see me coming, they flee like frightened animals. Or they pretend they do not know me."

The sad story brought tears to the eyes of Littlejohn, Scarlett, and Much.

Robin responded differently.

"Sit back down with me, Sir Knight." he requested. "There is still good wine here to be drunk. Tell me true, Sir. Are you positive there is no one who will lend you the sum you require?"

"My only hope is a miracle," the knight replied. "All I have is my faith on Our Dear Lady as security. She has never, ever, to this day, failed me."

Robin was a great devotee of Our Lady. He knew himself to be a sinner, but his faith overreached his guilt. The knight's mention of Our Lady quite touched him.

"That security I find to my liking," he told the knight. "I put my trust in Her more than in any person dwelling in all England.

"Littlejohn," Robin ordered. "Go to the treasury and fetch me four hundred pounds."

Littlejohn rejoiced in his heart to hear his master so request.

When he returned with the money, he urged Robin to further acts of charity.

"Master," he said. "This money is well lent. But we see the threadbare clothing the knight wears. We have yardage here that surpasses anything any merchant in the realm possesses. And what is more, our guest has such a spavined nag he makes a sorry impression. He must have one of our swift coursers."

"Yes," Robin agreed. "Let him have a gray courser. And a new saddle. For we now perceive that he is he is Our Lady's messenger."

Much added his idea.

"And he should also have a good palfrey."

"And a pair of decent boots," Will Scarlett added. "For he is a gentle knight."

"And I would add a pair of golden spurs," Littlejohn joined in. "That should take the lugubrious look off his face."

The knight showed his delight, but then asked the question about repayment.

"When, Master Robin, will you expect repayment for the sum you lend me?"

"On this very day of the month, in precisely one year," Robin told him. "I will be awaiting your arrival with four hundred pounds outside the door of our Barnsdale lodge."

The knight was attired by the Merrymen in his new robes and was given his two new horses and other gifts. As he was about to mount his courser, Robin added his final bounty.

"It would be shameful for a gentle knight to ride off to the abbey unaccompanied by squire, yeoman, or page. I lend you my boon companion, Littlejohn, to be your servant for the nonce."

Littlejohn was right happy to accompany the knight to retrieve his lands and goods.

The knight, accompanied by Littlejohn, rode off through the greenwood, heading for Barnsdale town and Watling Street towards the highway to York and Saint Mary's Abbey.

Nowe is the knyght gone on his way.
This game hym thought full gode.
Whan he loked on Bernysdale
He blessyd Robyn Hode.

And whan he thought on Bernysdale,
On Scarlok, Much and Johann,
He blessyd them for the best compani
That ever he in come.

Than spake that gentyll knyght,
To Lytell Johann gan he saye,

"To-morrowe I must to Yorke toune
To Seynt Mari abbay.

"And to the abbot of that place
Foure hundred pounde I must pay.
And but I be there upon this nyght
My londe is lost for ay."

The abbot sayd to his convent,
There he stode on grounde,
"Thys day twelfe moneth cam a knyght
And borrowed foure hundred pounde.

"He borrowed four hundred pounde
Upon his londe and fee.
But he come thys ylkë day
Disherited shall he be."

"It is full erely," sayd the pryoure.
The day is not yet ferre gone.
I had lever to pay an hondred pounde
And lay it downe anone.

The knyght is ferre beyond the see.
In Englonde is his right.
And suffereth honger and colde
And many a sori nyght.

"It were grete pytë," sayd the pryoure
"So to have his londe.
And ye be so lyght of your consyence,
Ye do to hym muche wronge."

"Thou arte ever in my berde," sayd the abbot,
"By God and Seynt Rycharde."
With that cam in a fat-heded monke,
The hye selerer.

"He is dede or hanged," sayd the monke,
"By God that bought me dere.
And we shall have to spende in this place
Foure hundred pounde by yere."

The abbot and the hye selerer
Stertë for the full bolde,
The hye justice of Englonde
The abbot there dyde holde.

The hye justice and many mo
Had taken into theyr honde
Holy all the knyghtes det
To put that knight to wronge.

They demed the knight onder sore,
The abbot and his meynë.
"But he come this ylkë day
Dysheryte shall he be."

"He wyll not come yet," sayde the justyce.
"I dare well undertake."
But in sorowe tymë for them all
The knyght came to the gate.

Than bespake that gentyll knyght
Untyll his meynë
"Now put on your simple wedes
That ye brought fro the see."

They put on their simple wedes.
They came to the gates anone.
The porter was redy hymselfe
And welcomed them everychone.

'Welcome, syr knyght," sayde the porter.
"My lorde to mete is he.
And so is many a gentyll man
For the love of the."

The porter swore a full grete othe.
"By God that made me,
Here be the best coresed hors
That ever yet sawe I me.

"Lede them in to the stable," he sayde
"That eased might they be."
"They shall not come therein" sayde the knight,

"By God that dyed on a tre."

Lordës were to mete isette
In that abbots hall.
The knight went forth and kneled downe,
And salued them grete and small.

"Do gladly, syr abbot," sayde the knyght.
"I am come to holde my day."
The first word that the abbot spoke,
"Hast thou brought my pay?"

"Not one peny," sayde the knyght,
"By God that maked me."
"Thou are a shrewed detour," sayde the abbot.
"Syr justice, drynke to me.

"What doost thou here," sayde the abbot.
"But thou haddest brought thy pay?"
"For God," than sayde the knyght,
"To pray of a longer daye."

"Thy daye is broke," sayde the justyce.
"Londe gettest thou none."
"Now, good syr justice, he be my frende
And fende me of my fone!"

"I am holde with the abbot," sayde the justyce,
"Both with cloth and fee."
"Now, good syr sheryfe, be my frende!"
"Nay, for God," sayde he.

"Now, good syr abbot, be my frende,
For thy curtysë.
And holde my londës in thy honde
Tyll I have made the gree!

"And I wyll be thy trewe servaunte,
And trewely serve the,
Tyll ye have foure hundred pounde
Of money gode and fre"

The abbot sware a full grete othe,

"By God that dyed on a tre,
Get thy londe where thou may,
For thou getest non of me."

"By dere worthy God," than sayde the knyght,
"That all this worldë wrought.
But I have my londe agayne,
Full dere it shal be bought.

"God, that was of mayden borne,
Leve us well to spede!
For it is good to assay a frende
Or that a man have need."

The abbot lothely on hym gan loke,
And vylaynesly hym gan call.
"Out," he sayd, "thou false knyght.
Spede the out of my hal!"

"Thou lyest," than sayde the gentyll knyght,
"Abbot, in thy hal.
False knyght was I never,
By God that made us al."

Up then stode that gentyll knyght.
To the abbot sayde he,
"To suffer a knyght to knele so longe
Thou canst no curteyseye.

"In iustes and in tournaments
Full ferre than have I be.
And put myself as ferre in prees
As ony that ever I see."

"What wyll ye gyve mere," sayde the justyce,
"And the knyght shall make a releyse?
And elles dar I safly swere
Ye holde never your londe in pees."

"An hundred pounde," sayd the abbot.
The justice sayd, "Gyve him two."
"Nay, be God," sayd the knyght,
"Ye get not my londe so.

"Though ye wolde gyve a thousand more,
Yet were ye never the nere.
Shal there never be myne ayre
Abbot, justyce ne frere."

He stert hym to a borde anone,
Tyll a table rounde.
And there he shoke oute of a bagge
Even four hundred pound.

"Have here thi golde, syr abbot," sayd the knyght,
"Which that thou lentest me.
Had thou ben curtyses at my comynge
I wolde have rewarded the."

The abbot sat styll and ete no more,
For all hys ryall fare.
He cast his hede on his shulder
And fast began to stare.

"Take me my golde again," sayd the abbot.
"Sir justyce, that I toke the."
"Not a peni," sayde the justice
"Bi God that dyed on tre."

"Syr abbot, and ye men of lawe,
Now have I holde my daye.
Now shal I have my londe agayne
For ought that you can saye."

The knyght stert out of the dore.
Awaye was all his care.
And on he put his good clothynge.
The other he lefte there.

He wente hym forth full mery syngynge,
As men have told in tale.
His lady met hym at the gate,
At home in Verysdale.

"Welcome, my lorde," sayde his lady.
"Syr, lost is all your good?"

"Be mery, dame," sayde the knyght,
"And pray for Robyn Hode,

"That ever his soule be in blysse.
He holpe me out of tene.
Ne had be his kyndënesse
Beggers had we bene.

"The abbot and I accorded ben.
He is served of his pay.
The gode yeman lent it me
As I cam by the way."

This knyght than dwelled fayre at home,
The soothe for to saye,
Tyll he had got four hundred pounde
Al redy for to pay.

He purveyed hym a hundred bowes,
The stryngs well ydyght,
An hundred shefe of arowes gode
The hedys burnished full bryght.

And every arowe al ellë long,
With pecok well idyght
Inocked all with white silver.
It was a seemly syght.

He purveyed him an hundred men,
Well harnessed in that stede
And hym selfe in that same suite,
And clothed in white and rede.

He bare a launsgay in his honde,
And a man ledde his male,
And redden with a lyght songe
Unto Bernysdale.

But at Wentbrydge there was a wrastelyng,
And there taryed was he.
And there was all the best yemen
Of all the weest contrë.

A full fayre game there was up set,
A white bulle up ipyght,
A grete courser, with sadle and brydil,
With golde burnyssht full bryght.

A payre of gloves, a rede golde rynge,
A pype of wyne, in fay.
What man that bereth hym best i-wys
The pryce shall bere away.

There was a yeman in that place,
And best worthy was he.
And for he was ferre and frembde bested
Slayne he sholde have be.

The knyght had ruthe of thys yeman,
In place where that he stode.
He sayde that yeman sholde have no harme,
For love of Robyn Hode.

The knight presed in to the place,
An hundredth followed hym fre
With bowes bent and arowes sharpe
For to shend that compani.

They shuldered all and made hym rome
To wete what he wolde say.
He toke the yeman bi the honde
And gave hym al the play.

He gave hym five marke for his wyne,
There it lay on the molde,
And bad it shulde be set a broche
Drynkë who so wolde.

Thus longe tarried this gentyll knyght,
Tyll that play was done.
So longe abode Robyn fastyinge
Thre ouris after the none.

A Gest of Robyn Hode
The Second Fytte

CHAPTER TEN

The Greedy Abbot

As the knight thought back on his Barnsdale stay, he was immensely grateful to Robin. And he also blessed Scarlet, Much, and John as the finest companions he had ever known.

Riding along with Littlejohn at his side, he explained "I must get to York town, to Saint Mary Abbey, by tomorrow. If I do not get to the abbot with the four hundred pounds in time, I will lose my lands and goods forever."

The next morning, at the abbey, the abbot was explaining his situation to the prior.

"A year ago a knight came here and borrowed four hundred pounds from me, signing over his properties and goods as collateral. Unless he comes here this very day with four hundred pounds in re-payment, his lands and goods are forfeit and become mine."

"It is still early in the day," the prior responded. "I would prefer to let him have his lands back for a hundred pounds. Otherwise he will be destitute, and will likely have to leave England. In that case, he will suffer countless indignities. Have you no conscience, Abbot? You clearly are doing the knight wrong."

"There you go, Prior," the abbot complained. "You're always in my beard[7]."

At that point, the pudgy cellarer[8] and the high justice entered the room.

---

7   In opposition to me.

8   A monk in a monastery who is responsible for maintaining the supply of food and drink.

The cellarer opined that the knight would not be coming to ransom his property.

"He is probably dead or hanged," was his verdict.

The high justice was wholly on the abbot's side.

"If the knight does not arrive this very day," he affirmed, "he will be legally dispossessed of his lands."

As the high justice was delivering his opinion, the knight rode up to the abbey gate.

He and Littlejohn changed into threadbare simple clothing before making their presence known.

Littlejohn rang the bell and the porter came to the gate and welcomed the arrivals.

The porter commented on what fine horses the knight and his squire rode and offered to stable them.

"No, good porter," the knight replied. "The horses will remain outside the gate while I have my meeting with the abbot."

He left Littlejohn with the steeds and was conducted by the porter to the refectory where the abbot was supping with the prior and the high justice.

The knight, when he entered, went down on his knees before the three dignitaries.

"I have come here, Sir Abbot, on the appointed day," he declared.

"Do you have my money?" the abbot demanded.

"Not even a penny of it," the knight responded.

"Then you are nothing but a damned debtor," the abbot spat out. "What in the world urged you to show your sorry face before me today without so much as a penny?"

"I have come," the knight pleaded, "to request an extension on my loan."

"Fie," exclaimed the justice. "Your time has run out. And that's the end of it."

"Oh please, Sir Justice," the knight urged. "I seek your friendship and legal defense against my foes."

"Not at all," quoth the justice. "I fully agree with the abbot's point. I see no reason to grant an extension."

The knight, still on his knees, made a final plea to the merciless abbot.

"I beg you on bended knee, Sir Abbot. If you will give me a bit more time, I will serve you any way you wish. I will be able to acquire the four hundred pounds if you will just show me some ruth."

"Get out of here, false knight!" the abbot spat. "Out of my hall – now!"

The knight got up off his knees and spoke severely to the abbot.

"You lie in your teeth, false abbot. I have never been, and am not now, a false knight. And to suffer a knight to kneel so long on this cold stone floor shows you to be a clergyman lacking in Christian charity. My bravery as a knight have I shown again and again in jousts, tournaments and in the fray of battle."

The justice intervened.

"Perhaps if you were to offer a bit of extra recompense the abbot might grant you a bit more time."

The abbot saw a chance to wring more out of the knight and immediately spoke up.

"A hundred pounds," he offered.

"That's not sufficient," the justice interrupted, thinking he might come in for a bit of this extortion himself. "I would say two hundred pounds would be more equitable."

The knight had tried both abbot and justice in his mind. It was time to bring his charade to an end.

"Not a hundred pounds. Not two hundred pounds. Not a thousand!" he enunciated grimly. "No abbot, no judge, and no friar will rob me of my land."

With that he turned about and shook the four hundred pounds he had borrowed from Robin onto a near-by table.

"I have tested your Christian charity and your sense of justice on the scale of morality," he said. "And you, false abbot and you, perfidious justice, have been found wanting

"There is the gold you lent me, paid in full. And if you had not proved an avaricious and hypocritical clergyman, I would certainly have rewarded you with more."

The abbot and the justice were taken aback.

The knight turned heel and strode out of the hall.

Once out the door and beyond the gate, he and Littlejohn discarded their plain clothes and donned the garb they had traveled in.

The knight thanked Littlejohn for his help. And Littlejohn, well pleased with the outcome of their journey, took leave of the knight and returned to Barnsdale.

The once doleful knight sang merrily as he traversed the roads and trails to his home in Veresdale. When he arrived, his lady met him at the gate.

"Welcome, my lord," she greeted him. "Have we, indeed, lost everything we owned?"

"Cheer up, my dear," the knight replied. "And pray for Robin Hood. Had it not been for his kindness we would be beggars at this moment. I have paid back the abbot with gold lent to me by that good yeoman of Barnsdale."

Now, even with his lands and goods restored, the knight took close to a year to acquire the four hundred pounds he owed Robin. And he raised more to boot in order to return to Barnsdale with gifts aplenty.

He purchased a hundred well-strung bows and a hundred sheaves of fine, burnished-headed arrows. Every arrow was an ell long, dighted with peacock feathers and notched with silver. It was a most impressive assortment.

He gathered together a hundred men and liveried them in red and white.

Bearing a lance in hand, he led his band merrily towards Barnsdale a few days before he was to meet with Robin and return the money he had borrowed.

But when the merry troop got as far as Wentbridge, there was a festive entertainment in progress.

A large crowd had gathered for a wrestling match. The prizes offered were a white bull, a great courser with saddle and bridle, a pair of gloves, and a gold ring.

An outlander had come to Wentbridge to participate in the match. And he proved a contender who outperformed all the locals.

First, he won the gold ring.

He was then challenged by one of the local favorites and won the gloves.

The crowd grew restless. It was not expected that a stranger would out-perform the locals.

The knight was intrigued by the skill of the winner, but was alarmed at the mounting displeasure of the crowd.

The next prize to be won was the saddled horse.

A strapping Wentbridge lad challenged the stranger. At issue was not only the valuable horse but the honor of Wentbridge itself. As the local and the outsider struggled in the ring, the knight heard oaths hurled at the stranger. One of the locals was suggesting to his neighbors that if the stranger won, what he would receive as a prize would be not a courser but a hanging by the mob.

The crowd grew restive and took a dislike towards the stranger who had arrived on the scene. Threats were made against him.

The knight was in mind of the courtesy Robin Hood had shown him and took pity on the yeoman and swore that no harm should come to the fellow.

He assembled his hundred men with bows drawn and arrows nocked to quell the crowd.

When the stranger overcame his opponent, the mob grew restive indeed. The knight rode into the ring and announced to the throng that his men would unleash their arrows on any and all who attempted to harm the stranger. He ordered that the prize horse be brought forth and had the winner mount.

As the stranger rode through the grumbling crowd and away into the greenwood, the knight further addressed the crowd.

"Let the wrestling match continue, confined to the good burgers of Wentbridge and its surroundings. And when the white bull has been fairly won, I invite all of you to enjoy your fill of ale and wine at yonder tavern. And I myself will pay for drinks for each and every person gathered here.

The crowd was appeased. The match continued, following which a merry time was had by the formerly disgruntled crowd.

Peace reigned again in Wentbridge. The wrestling contest occupied the interest of the gathering. Following which, there was tippling, guzzling and even toasts to the knight who provided the flow of liquors.

The knight tarried in Wentbridge to enjoy the proceedings.

"Go we to dyner," sayd Lytell Johann.
Robyn Hode sayd, "Nay.
For I drede Oure Lady be wroth with me,
For she sent me nat my pay."

"Have no dout, Maister," sayde Lytell Johann.
"Yet is not the sonne at rest.
For I dare say, and savely swere
The knight is trewe and truste."

"Take thy bowe in honde," sayde Robyn.
"Late Much wende with the,
And so shal Willyam Scarlok,
And no man abyde with me.

"And walke up under the Sayles
And to Watlynge-strete,
And wayte after some unkuth gest
Up-chaunce ye may them mete.

Whether he be messangere
Or a man that myrthës can,
Of my gode he shal have som
Yf he be a pore man."

Furth than stert Lytell Johann
Half in tray and tene,
And gyred hym with a full gode swerde
Under a mantel of grene.

They went up to the Sayles,
Thes yemen all thre.
They loked est, they loked weest.
They myght no man se.

But as they loked in Bernysdale,
By the hyë waye,
Than were they ware of two blacke monkes,
Eche on a gode palferay.

Than bespake Lytell Johann,
To Much he gan say,
"I dare lay my lyfe to wedde
These monkes have brought oure pay.

"Make glad chere," sayde Lytell Johann,
And frese our bowes of ewe,
And loke your hertes be seker and sad
Your strynges trusty and trewe.

"The monke hath two and fifty men,
And seven somers full stronge.
There rydeth no bysshop in this londe
So ryally, I understond.

"Brethren," sayde Lytell Johann
"Here are noo more but we thre.
But we brynge them to dyner
Our maister dare we not se.

"Bende your bowes," sayd Lytell Johann.
"Make all yon prese to stoned.
The formost monke, his lyfe and his deth
Is closed in my honde.

"Abyde, chore monke," sayde Lytell Johann,
"Noo ferther that thou gone.
Yf thou doost, be dere worthi God,
Thy deth is in my honde.

"And evyll thryfte on thy hede," sayde Lytell Johann
"Ryght under thy hates bonde.
For thou hast made our maister wroth,

He is fastynge so longe."

"Who is your maister?" sayde the monke.
Lytell Johann sayde, "Robyn Hode.
"He is a stronge thefe," syd the monke.
"Of hym herd I never gode."

"Thou lyest," than sayde Lytell Johann.
"And that shal rewë the.
He is a yeman of the forest.
To dyne he hath bode the.

Much was redy with a bolte,
Redly and anone
He set the monke to-fore the brest,
To the gounde that he can gone.

Of two and fifty wyght yonge yemen
There abode not one,
Saf a lytell page and a grome,
To lede the somers with Lytell Johann.

They brought the monke to the lodge-dore
Whether he were loth or lefe,
For to speke with Robyn Hode,
Maugre in theyr tethe.

Robyn dyde a downe his hode,
The monke whan that he se.
The monke was not so curteyse,
His hode then let he be.

"He is a chorl, maister, by dere worthi God,"
Than sayd Lytell Johann.
"Thereof no force," sayd Robyn.
"For curteyse can he none.

"How many meyne," sayde Robyn,
"Had this monke, Johann?"
"Fyfty and two whan that we met,
But many of them be gone."

"Let blowe a horne," sayd Robyn,
"That felawshyp may us knowe."
Seven score of wyght yemen
Came pryckynge on a rowe.

And erytch of them a good mantel
Of scarlet and of raye.
All they came to good Robyn
To wyte what he wolde say.

They made the monke to wasshe and wype,
And syt at his dynere.
Robyn Hode and Lytell Johann
They serve him both in-fere.

"Do gladly, monke," sayde Robyn.
"Gramercy, syr," sayde he.
"Where is your abbay, whan ye are at home,
And who is your avowë?"

Seynt Mari Abbay," sayde the monke,
"Though I be simple here."
"In what office?" sayd Robyn.
"Syr, the hye selerer."

"Ye be the mere welcom," sayde Robyn,
"So ever mote I the.
Fyll of the best wyne," sayd Robyn.
"This monke shall drynke to me.

"But I have grete mervayle," sayde Robyn,
"Of all this longë day
I drede Our Lady be wroth with me,
She sent me not my pay."

"Have no dout, maister," sayde Lytell Johann.
"Ye have no need, I saye.
This monke hath brought it, I dare well swere
For he is of her abbay."

"And she was a borowe," sayde Robyn,
"Betwene a knyght and me.
Of a lytell money that I hym lent

Under the grene-wode tre.
"And yf thou hast that sylver ibrought,
I pray the let me se,
And I shall helpë the eftsones
If thou have need to me."

The monke swore a full grete othe,
With a sory chere.
"Of the borowehode thou spekest to me
Herde I never ere."

"I make myn avowe to God," sayde Robyn,
"Monke, thou art to blame,
For God is holde a ryghtwys man,
And so is his dame.

"Thou toldest with thyn owne tonge,
Thou may not say nay,
How thou arte her servaunt,
And servest her every day.

"And thou art made her messangere.
Mi money for to pay,
Therefore I cun the more thanke
Thou arte come at thy day.

"What is in your cofers?" sayde Robyn.
"Trewe than tell thou me."
"Syr," he sayd, "Twenty marke,
All so mote I the."

"Yf there be no mere," sayde Robyn,
"I wyll nat one peny.
Yf thou hast myster of ony more,
Syr, mere I shall lende to the."

"And yf I fynde more," sayde Robyn,
"I-wys thou shalte it for gone,
For of thy spendynge-sylver, monke,
Thereof wyll I ryght non.

"Go nowe forthe, Lytell Johann,
And the trouth tell thou me.
If there be no mere but twenty marke,
No peny that I se."

Lytell Johann spred his mantel downe,
As he had done before.
And he tolde out of the monkes male
Eyght hundred pounde and more.

Lytell Johan let it lye full styll
And went to his maister in hast.
"Syr," he sayde, "The monke is trewe inowe,
Our lady hath doubled your cast."

"I make myn avowe to God," sayde Robyn.
"Monke, what tolde I the?
Oure Lady is the trewest woman
That ever yet founde I me.

"By dere worthi God," sayde Robyn,
"To sech all Englond throrow,
Yet founde I never to my pay
A moche better borowe.

"Fyll of the best wyne, and do hym drynke," sayde Robyn.
"And grete well thy landy hende.
And yf she have need to Robyn Hode
A frende she shall hym fynde.

"And yf she nedeth ony mere sylver,
Come thou agayne to me.
And, by this token she hath me sent
She shal have such thre."

The monke was goynge to London ward,
There to hold grete mote.
The knight that rode so hye on hors
To brynge hym under fote.

"Whether be ye away?" sayd Robyn.
"Syr, to maners in this londe,
Too reken with our reves
That have done moch wronge."

"Come now forth, Lytell Johann
And harken to my tale.
A better yeman I knowe none
To seke a monkës male."

"How moch is in yonder other coffer?" sayde Robyn.
"The soth must we se."
"By Oure Lady," than sayde the monke,
"That were no curteysye.

"To bydde a man to dyner,
And syth hym bete and bynde."
"It is our olde maner," sayde Robyn,
'To leve but lytell behynde."

The monke toke the hors with spore,
No lenger wolde he abyde.
"Aske to drynke," than sayd Robyn,
"Or that ye forther ryde."

"Nay, for God," than sayde the monke,
"Me reweth I cam so nere.
For better chepe I might have dyned
In Blithe or Dankestere."

"Grete well your abbot," sayde Robyn,
"And your pryour, I you pray.
And byd hym send me such a monke
To dyner every day."

Now lete we that monke be styll
And speke we of that knight.
Yet he came to holde this day
Whyle that it was lyght.

He dyde him streyt to Bernysdale,
Under the grene-wode tre.
And he founde there Robyn Hode

And all his mery meynë.

The knyght lyght doune of his good palfrey,
Robyn whan he gan se.
So curteysly he dyde adoune his hode
And set him on his kne.

"God the save, Robyn Hode
And all this compani."
"Welcome be thou, gentyll knight,
And right welcome to me."

Than bespake hym Robyn Hode
To that knight so fre.
"What need dryveth the to grene-wode?
I praye the, syr knight, tell me.

"And welcome be thou, gentyll knight.
Why hast thou be so longe?"
"For the abbot and the hye justyce
Wolde have had my londe."

"Hast thou thy londe agayne?" sayde Robyn.
"Treuth than tell thou me."
"Ye, for God," sayde the knyght,
"And that thanke I God and the.

"But take no grefe, that I have be so longe,
I came by a wrastelynge.
And there I holpe a pore yeman
With wronge was put behynde."

"Nay, for God," sayd Robyn.
"Syr knyght, that thanke I the.
What man that helpeth a good yeman
His frende than wyll I be."

"Have here foure hundred pounde," sayde the knyght,
"The whiche ye lent to me.
And here is also twenty marke
For your curteyse."

"Nay, for God," sayde Robyn,

"Thou broke it well for ay.
For Oure Lady, by her hye selerer
Hath sent to me my pay.

"And yf I toke it i-twyse,
A shame it were to me.
But trewely, gentyll knight
Welcome arte thou to me."

Whan Robyn had tole his tale
He loughe and made gode chere.
"By my trouthe," then sayde the knyght,
"Your money is redy here."

"Broke it well," sayd Robyn.
"Thou gentyll knight so fre.
And welcome be thou, gentyll knight
Under my trystell-tre.

"But what shall these bowes do?" sayde Robyn.
"And these arowes ifedred fre?"
"By God," than sayde the knyght,
"A pore present to the."

"Come now forth, Lytell Johann,
And go to my treasure,
And brynge me there foure hundred pounde
The monke over-told it me.

"Have here foure hundred pounde,
Thou gentyll knyght and trewe.
And bye the hors and harness gode,
And gylte thy spores all newe.

"And yf thou fayle ony spendynge,
Com to Robyn Hode,
And by my trouth thou shalt none fayle,
The whyles I have any gode.

"And broke well thy foure hundred pound
Whiche I lent to the,
And make thy selfe no more so bare
By the counsel of me."

Thus than holpe hym gode Robyn
The knight all of his care.
God that syt in heven hye
Graunte us well to fare!

The Gest of Robyn Hode
The Fourth Fytte
Circa 1300 A.D.

CHAPTER ELEVEN

The Lying Monk

But back in Barnsdale, Robin was awaiting the knight and grew restive. It was three hours after noon and there was no sign of the knight. Robin would not take meat for he trusted Our Lady to respond to the loan he had made to the knight one year previous, to the day.

Littlejohn was urging Robin to eat.

"No, John," Robin replied. "I fear that Our Lady is upset with me for some reason. Otherwise she would have sent me my pay. I will not sup until she sends me money, gold, or jewels. Or lacking that, at least a guest to join me at table."

The day is not yet over," Littlejohn noted. "I still believe the knight will be true to his trust."

Robin required a sign – a guest to replenish the treasury or one who would have need of charity. If Our Lady was not going to send the knight, then might she not send another guest in his place?

To Littlejohn Robin ordered, "Arm yourself with bow and arrow. And take both Much and Will Scarlet towards Barnsdale. Tarry in Wattling Street and see whether a guest might appear to join my table. If he should turn out to be a poor man, he shall not pay a penny for his fare."

Littlejohn, Much the miller's son, and Will Scarlet left Robin to his solitude and proceeded to encounter a guest who might lighten their master's mood.

When they arrived in Barnsdale, they looked high and low for a guest that Our Lady would show unto them.

And there, coming down the highway, they spied two Blackfriar monks approaching on their palfreys.

Littlejohn nudged Much. "I do believe the pay we were here to collect is riding astride yon palfreys. Get your bow strung and in readiness. The head monk has a retinue of fifty two yeomen and seven pack horses. Methinks we are about to bag treasure beyond whatever even a bishop might bear."

When the head monk drew near to the outlaws, Littlejohn addressed him politely.

"Our master bids you and the two of us to join him at dinner."

To the cortege following the monk, Littlejohn shouted: "You had best disperse. I hold the life or death of your black-clad leader in my hand. Our master has been fasting for three hours awaiting the company of your leader to sup with him. The rest of you best scatter."

"Who might this master of yours be?" asked the monk.

"His name is Robin Hood," answered Littlejohn. "And he is growing quite wroth that you have caused him to delay his meal so long."

"Robin Hood!" scoffed the monk. "I have heard of him. But never so much as a good word. He is nothing but a common thief and a blackguard."

"You lie in your teeth, you churl of a monk," Littlejohn exploded. "Master Robin is a yeoman of the forest. And he has invited you to dine with him."

Much aimed a bolt at the monk's chest and ordered him off his horse.

As the monk dismounted, fifty of the troop turned tail and scattered away in every direction. Only a little page and a groom remained to attend to their master.

Littlejohn and Much led the friar into the forest. The page and the groom followed with the horse.

When they got to the lodge door, Robin was waiting outside.

Robin lowered his hood in courteous greeting to his guest. The surly monk defiantly left his own in place.

"This monk is a churl, Master," Littlejohn declared.

"It makes no difference," Robin answered. "Some people simply do not have any manners."

Robin went on to ask Littlejohn how many men had accompanied the monk.

"There were fifty-two," Littlejohn told him. "But most fled when they realized what was happening."

"It is well," Robin decided. "Blow the horn to assemble our men. We have our guest. It is time we ate."

Much blew his bugle and seven score lusty yeomen came bounding and jostling into the trysting lea.

Rather than being attired in their Lincoln green, the men were festively dressed in striped scarlet clothing.

They washed hands and face in the creek, making sure the monk did the same. Then all sat to dine.

Robin and Littlejohn both served the monk with considerable

courtesy.

The monk warmed up to Robin as he was presented with the tasty edibles and he fell into a feeling of camaraderie with the troop of good yeomen he had joined at table.

Robin asked him what his home abbey was and what his function was there.

"I serve as cellarer at Saint Mary's Abbey," the friar explained.

"Then you are doubly welcome here," Robin enthused. "You indeed bring good fortune to me."

Robin called to Pym to bring forth the best wine for the messenger from Our Lady.

"All day long," Robin explained, "I have been concerned that Our Lady was angry with me. I was beginning to think she would not send me the repayment I was expecting."

"There's no longer any reason to worry about that, now, is there master?" Littlejohn noted. "This monk comes from her abbey. He clearly has brought the repayment from her with him."

"Yes," Robin agreed. "She was the security between a knight and me for money I lent him here."

To the monk he said, "If you brought silver with you, hand it over to me. And, in return, if you ever have need of anything from me in the future, just let me know."

The friar expressed his displeasure with a great oath.

"This is absolute nonsense you are speaking," he declared. "I have never heard of any borrowing or lending that has anything to do with me."

"I swear to God, Monk," Robin replied, "that you are simply misinformed. Just as God is true to the righteous, so is his Dame.

"You told me yourself you are her servant. And as cellarer you serve her daily. Consequently, it's clear you are her messenger and have brought me the reimbursement from her this very day. So I really must thank you. Tell me truly, then, monk. How much do you have in your coffers?"

The monk put on his sincerest look.

"Sir," he declared. "All I have is twenty marks. I will gladly give all that to you."

"If there is no more than that," Robin declared, "I will not touch one penny of it. And if you need more, I will gladly lend it to you. But if there is more than twenty marks, I will have to keep the surplus, leaving you your twenty marks as spending money.

"So, Littlejohn, go take a look in the good friar's coffers. Come back and tell me if there is only twenty marks there. If so, I don't want to see so much as a penny of it."

Littlejohn went to the monk's coffers, spread his mantle on the ground, and poured the contents of the wallet he found onto the cloth.

He was delighted to count more than eight hundred pounds. He returned to Robin with the good news.

"Master," he said. "The monk turns out to be a true messenger from Our Lady. And she has doubled your investment."

"By God, Sir Monk," Robin exclaimed. "What did I tell you? There is no more reliable lady anywhere in the realm. There is no better investment than one secured by Her.

"Come," he continued. "Let the friar drink deeply of our finest wine. And let all know that if Saint Mary needs any more silver invested through Her by me, this token she has sent assures that I shall respond threefold."

The Blackfriar was not made happy by Robin Hood's enthusiasm for the Virgin, and expressed a desire to be on his way as soon as possible to proceed on to London to attend a meeting he had been heading for there.

"It is a coarse matter," the monk said to Robin, "to invite a man to dinner and then to take him for all he is worth."

"However," Robin told him, "that is precisely our way. We always leave a little of the loot behind so our guests don't leave us empty handed.

"But must you rush away so soon?" he continued. "Why don't you stay a while longer and join us for a few more drinks?"

"No, thank you," the monk scowled. "I just wish I had never come near this place. The bill runs a bit high. I could have dined in Blythe or Doncaster for a lot less."

As the sad monk rode off, Robin shouted after him: "Be sure to give our best regards to your abbot. And to the prior as well, of course. And ask them to send as fine a monk as you to join us for dinner every day."

And as the monk rides away out of the greenwood, let us turn our attention to the knight.

He saw that it was getting late and needed to be on his way to Barnsdale.

He arrived at the Great Oak and found Robin and his Merrymen all there.

As the knight dismounted from his palfrey, Robin lowered his hood in greeting.

Robin inquired whether the abbot and the high justice had relinquished his land back to him.

"Thanks be to God, to Our Lady, and to you, Robin," the knight exclaimed. "I have all my lands and goods back again.

"But I want you to know why I have arrived here at this late hour. On my way here, I observed a wrestling-match where a poor yeoman, a stranger to the area, was being unjustly set upon by the locals. So I stopped there to help the poor fellow."

"You did right," Robin told him. "I always approve of anyone who will go out of his way to assist a good yeoman."

The knight pulled out his wallet.

"And here," he said, "are the four hundred pounds you lent me. With an additional twenty marks for your generosity."

"No, sir," Robin protested. "You keep all that. Because Our Lady has already repaid me through a visit by her high cellarer. If I took the amount from you, it would be a shameful act. Truly, gentle knight, it is enough that you have come here this appointed day."

Robin laughed loud at the turn of events. But the knight protested.

"No," he said. "This money is yours. I insist you take it."

"It is a closed case," quoth Robin. "Enjoy that money. It is not mine and I cannot take it in good faith. Enjoy it well. And again, I say to you, 'welcome back to our company.'"

Robin then observed the bows and arrows the knight had brought with him.

"What are those bows and feathered arrows all about?" he asked.

"They are a very poor present I have brought to you, Robin."

"A kind and generous offer," Robin responded.

"Littlejohn, go over to the treasury and bring me the four hundred pound over-payment the monk left with us."

When Littlejohn returned with the sum, Robin handed it to the knight.

"Here, Sir Knight," he said. "Take this four hundred pounds and buy yourself a decent horse and harness. And re-gild your spurs. And if, for any reason, you have need of anything more, you shall not lack so long as I have resources.

"And, by all means, get yourself outfitted in merrier style than you came here in."

And that is the manner in which Robin Hood helped the gentle, honest knight.

Robyn sawe the busshement to-broke,
In grene wode he wolde have be.
Many an arowe there was shot
Amonge that compani.

Lytell Johann was hurte full sore
With an arowe in he kne,
That he might neyther go nor ryde.
It was full grete pytë.

"Maister," then sayd Lytell Johann,
"If ever thou lovedst me,
And for that ylkë lordës love
That dyed upon a tree,

"And for the medes of my service
That I have served the,
Let never the proud sheryfe
Alyve now fyndë me.

"But take out thy browne swerde
And smyte all of my hede,
And gyve me woundës depe and wyde.
No lyfe on me be lefte."

"I wolde nat that," sayde Robyn,
"Johann, that thou were slawe,
For all the golde in mery Englonde,
Though it lay now on a rawe."

God forbede," sayde Lytell Much,
"That dyed on a tre,
That thou sholdest, Lytell Johann
Parte our compani."

Up he toke hym on his backe
And bare hym well a myle.
Many a tyme he layd him downe
And shot another whyle.

Then was there a fayre castell
A lytell within the wode.
Double-dyched it was about,
And walled, by the rode.

And there dwelled that gentyll knyght,
Syr Rycharde at the Lee
That Robyn had lent his gode
Under the grene-wode tre.

In he toke gode Robyn
And all his compani.
"Welcom be thou, Robyn Hode.

Welcom art thou to me.

"And moche I thanke the of thy comfort,
And of thy curteysye,
And of thy grete kindness
Under the grene-wode tre.

"I love no man in all this worlde
So much as I do the.
For all the proud sheryf of Notyngham
Right here shalt thou be.

Shutte the gates and draw the bridge,
And let noo man come in.
And arme you well and make you redy,
And to the walles ye wynne.

"For one thynge, Robyn, I the behote.
I swere by Seynt Quyntyne,
These forty dayes thou wonnest with me
For soupe, ete, and dyne.

Bordes were layde, and clothes were spredde
Redely and anone.
Robyn Hode and his merry men
To metë can they gone.

A Gest of Robyn Hode
The Fyfth Fytte
Circa 1300 A.D.

Lythe and listin, gentylmen,
And herkyn to your songe,
Howe the proude sheryfe of Notyngham
And men of armys stronge,

Full fast cam to the hye sheryfe,
The contrë up to route.
And they besette the knyghtes castell,
The wallës all aboute.

The proude sheryfe loude gan crye,
And sayde, "Thou traytour knyght
Thou kepest here the kynges enemys
Agaynst the law and ryght.

"Syr, I wyll avow that I have done
The dedys that here be dyght
Upon all the landes that I have
As I am a trewe knyght.

"Wende furth, syrs, on your way
And do no mere to me
Tyll ye wyte oure kyngës wille
What he wyll say to the."

The sheryfe thus had his answere
Without any lesynge.
Forth he yede to London towne
All for to tel our kynge.

Ther he telde him of that knight,
And eke of Robyn Hode.
And also of the bolde archeres
That were soo noble and gode.

"He wyll avowe that he hath done
To mayntene the outlawes stronge.
He wyll be lorde, and set you at nought
In all the northe londe."

I wyl be at Notyngham," sayde oure kynge,
"Within this fourteenyght,
And take I wyll Robyn Hode

And so I wyll that knyght.

"Go nowe home sheryfe," sayde our kynge,
"And do as I byd the.
And ordeyn gode archers ynouwe
Of all the wyde contrë."

The sheryfe had his leve i-take
And went hym on his way.
And Robyn Hode to grene wode
Upon a certen day.

And Lytell Johann was hole of the arowe
That shot was in his kne.
And dyd hym streyght to Robyn Hode
Under the grene-wode tre.

A Gest of Robyn Hode
The Sixth Fytte
Circa 1300 A.D.

CHAPTER TWELVE

Sir Richard Harbors Some Fugitives

Robin Hood and Littlejohn were feeling an acute discomfort. They sorely missed the comfort of feminine companionship.

Robin was accustomed to relieving his condition by taking himself off to Nottingham to visit his lady love, Maid Marian.

Littlejohn was considering a visit to the bawdyhouse in Sayles. He had patronized the establishment on numerous occasions and had found it to his liking

"Have you ever considered partaking of Maken's charms at the Blue Boar?" Robin asked his lieutenant.

"Master Eadom's nut-brown ale has often slaked my thirst," John replied. "And Mistress Hyacinth's pasties have delighted my palate. But I have not, so far, sampled the delights offered by Maken the serving wench. Would you recommend what she has to offer, Robin?"

Robin smiled in remembrance as he recalled the visits he had made to the shack that stood behind the inn.

"Maken is unlike the ladies in Sayles," Robin revealed. "The bawds in Sayles welcome any visitor who carries a purse. Maken is not a bawd. She refuses more would-be customers than she accepts. And she, not the customer, determines the form of entertainment offered on any particular occasion. Since you are well-favored physically, Littlejohn, I doubt that Maken would refuse you. And you certainly will enjoy full value in exchange for the angel she receives for her services."

Littlejohn pondered the situation. The bawdyhouse of Sayles would offer relief but no new adventure. He had found Maken a comely and lively wench when she had served him his ale at the Blue Boar's tables.

"You say you are presently heading for Nottingham town to woo your lady-love," Littlejohn said.

"Just so, my friend," Robin replied.

"And you will pass the Blue Boar on the way?"

"And of course, I will stop off to quaff a pint or two."

"Then, Master, I will accompany you as far as the Blue Boar. And will partake of mine host's humming ale with you. What may transpire after that, no man can truly know."

The two outlaws laughed a hearty guffaw, picked up their staffs and headed for the highway. Each carried a horn, a bow and a quiver of arrows for protection. Should any mischief await either on his trek, a call on the horn would likely fetch the aid of any of the Merrymen who might be moving about in the greenwood and the bows and arrows and swords should any enemies intrude on their adventure.

As the merry companions headed up the hot and dusty Lincoln Highway towards Nottingham, their lust to slake the thirst of their gullets and their balls increased. By the time they reached the Sign of the Blue Boar, their thirst would first to be attended to.

Could not the needs of their balls find equal comfort next?

They were heartily greeted by mine host and led to a rustic table situated in the shade of a mighty oak. Hardly had they rested their bones on a bench when Maken's lively smile greeted them.

"By my halidom," the wench laughed. "It is the wickedest knaves in the shire who have come to drink us dry. Will it be one or two tankards each of the Blue Boar's finest ale?"

"I would as lief extract a kiss from that saucy mouth as any drink in good King Richard's kingdom," Littlejohn responded.

"I would serve ale or wine to any yeoman with the price to pay," Maken answered. "As to kisses, or any other personal services for that matter, I am more particular by far."

"You have served my companion, Littlejohn, scores of times, Maken." Robin interjected. "Tell me true, Lass. Do you find him comely or marred?"

"Let him stand up, fair Robin, that I may make judgment," Maken demanded.

After eyeing Littlejohn up and down, Maken gave her opinion.

"I have observed many a yeoman in my time," she declared. "And yea, may a nobleman as well. This giant, although rough hewn, is fair enough of face. In size, he is a man and a half. And muscled is he like a Saxon god.

"Since he is not attired in tights as are you and all your other men, I cannot fairly judge whether his peter corresponds in grandeur."

Robin answered her:

"In the greenwood, Maken, Littlejohn and I oft piss against the same tree. And mine eyes have occasionally caught sight of his prick as it spews forth enormous fountains of piss.

"You well know, from intimate experience, how nobly I am hung."

Maken smiled at Robin in sincere acknowledgement.

"I can assure you, Maken," he continued, "that the name Littlejohn could not apply to his massive tool. That organ could rightly be yclept John the Magnificent."

Maken chortled as she imagined what wonders might lurk beneath Littlejohn's trousers.

Then her smile faded and in a hushed voice she said:

"But, soft. Sit you down, Littlejohn. Master Eadom is eyeing me askance. He would rather see his guests drinking or supping than gossiping with the help. If either of you wished to discuss country matters with me, let it be over a tankard or two."

Robin and Littlejohn laughed and ordered two tankards each of humming ale.

When Maken returned with the order, Littlejohn spoke for himself.

"Master Robin is off to see his paramour in the town. And I am left here to solace myself. I will down both my two tankards and those of fair Robin myself. However ale and pasties will hardly assuage my lusts."

"And what might you be proposing, then, Littlejohn," Maken asked with a twinkle.

"I would join you in your parlor behind the inn," Littlejohn told her.

"Such companionship does not come harbingered with mere words," Maken smiled.

"Might it take an angel?" Littlejohn asked.

"Drink ye deep, then Littlejohn," Maken told him. "An angel will suffice nicely. But I must needs see whether Mistress Hyacinth will have time available to cover my serving duties. I will return anon to let you know how blows the wind."

Robin had earlier relieved his thirst and taken up his staff. He had bid adieu to his boon companion. He was quite sure of the way the wind was likely to blow for Littlejohn. And he had fish of his own to fry.

So, his staff in his hand, a whistle on his lips, and a hardon in his tights, Robin set out alone on the road to Nottingham town.

Once inside the town gates, Robin was able to arrive at Marian's cottage undetected by the proud sheriff or his constables. He knew the byways and alleys well that led to the dwelling of his true-love.

Maid Marian greeted her Robin with love and kisses. She set a crock of October ale on the table along with some tasty cakes and the couple made merry in the kitchen.

After laughs aplenty, the lovers retired to the bedroom for additional sport.

Maid Marian was ready for Robin. And the throbbing within Robin's tights promised that he was ready for her.

When they had disrobed and Robin's cock was winking merrily at Marian's turgid nipples, he was ready to precipitously mount her.

His recent period of lack of nookie had been pestering him mightily.

But Marian had been thinking of Robin's visit and had devised the form of lovemaking she now suggested.

"Robin," she said sweetly. "A good fuck in my bed is a wondrous and wild occasion. And I know it is what you most enjoy of all activities possible.

"And, we will enjoy such jolly fucking for as much time as you can recover from your sweet spurts.

"But first, I would that you indulge me with an alternative carnal experience."

Robin, always the gentleman and avidly content to accommodate to a lady's request, assented before even hearing what Maid Marian had to propose.

"What I desire as our first course this morning is to lie flat on my back on the bed.

"I would then like you to set yourself atop me with your tongue aimed at my dripping snatch and your pecker aimed at my salivating mouth.

"Then, let us taste each other until each has come with a resounding spasm."

Robin needed no further encouragement.

The two soon had arranged themselves for simultaneous cocksucking and cunt licking.

As Marian had hoped for, they each came to a "resounding spasm."

Thereafter, when his prick had regained its stiffness, the couple did, indeed, fuck in the manner that most pleased Robin. But it should not be imagined that he had not been enormously pleased, as well, by the simultaneous fellatio and cunnilingus.

It was much later before they were sated with lovemaking.

Robin had recently been considering how much happier he would be if he did not have to wend his long way to Nottingham town to see his paramour. If he could convince Maid Marian to come live the sylvan life in the forest, they could enjoy nightly congress. He would go so far as to consider marriage if need be. Friar Tuck would, he knew, be delighted to tie the bonds.

So, when they had their fill of carnal joys, Robin made the suggestion to Marian, concluding by asking her "What think you of the sylvan life?"

"As you know, Robin," she replied. "I enjoy outings into the greenwood. Gathering flowers and herbs there is a true delight. But dwelling in such rustic surroundings befits the more rugged sex. I love you dearly, with all my heart. And I am as true to you as you to me. But I find it hard to envision myself living amidst seven score rowdy outlaws in some forest cottage without benefit of the conveniences of the town."

Robin played, then, what he thought his most convincing argument.

"Yes," he agreed. "You would be surrounded by seven score merry men who would protect you with their very lives. But you would be wedded to only one. Friar Tuck could join us in holy wedlock. God and Our Dear Lady would bless our union. And you could ride to market any time you pleased to secure any of the amenities Nottingham, Barnsdale, or even Lincoln can provide. Do come to the greenwood to live with me and be my wife."

Maid Marian did her best not to reveal her true reaction to Robin's suggestion. She had been born and raised in town. She found her life there most comfortable. She was in love with her Robin. But she enjoyed the romantic fruits of that relationship in the comfort of her cottage.

When Robin left Marian's abode to head back down the highway, all he had in the way of commitment from his paramour concerning living with him in bucolic bliss was, "I will think on it."

It wasn't a yes. But, then again, neither was it a no.

On his return trek down the highway, as he approached the Blue Boar, Robin sensed something was dreadfully amiss.

He did not enter the inn boldly, but slid in stealthily.

Master Eadom greeted Robin with concerned visage.

"Soft, Master Robin," he cautioned. "Your good companion, whom you left here earlier in the day, tarried, enjoying his tankards, Mistress Hyacinth's pies, and…such enjoyments as any good yeoman craves.

"He had not left the premises more than a quarter hour when a score of the sheriff's men came thundering down the highway. The lead constable told me that a large outlaw of your band had been spotted disporting himself here. He asked me which way the man had gone.

"I, of course, denied ever seeing such a person. The constable swore a great oath at me and led his men at full gallop down the highway in the direction towards which Littlejohn had headed. I fear your friend may be in grave danger."

Robin thanked the host for the information and hastened down the highway to try to intercept Littlejohn.

Very shortly, Robin heard a ruckus. He escaped into the greenwood to observe, unobserved, what was afoot.

And what he saw was a skirmish. A score of men from his band surrounded Littlejohn. And they were exchanging arrow shots with the sheriff's men who had been sent to capture their stout companion.

It was clear that when Littlejohn had become aware of his pursuers' ambush, he had blown his horn, fetching a group of greenclad fellows to his aid.

Robin strung his bow and observed that a contingent of his Merrymen had caught the constables by surprise as they killed one, wounded two, and caused the remainder to turn tail and retreat. Robin stepped out of his hidingplace and joined his men in shooting arrows at the retreating lawmen.

None of the men who had responded to Littlejohn's bugle call had been wounded. However, the same could not be said for Littlejohn himself. An arrow from one of the lawmen had hit his knee and he was in great pain.

The sheriff's men regrouped down the road and turned back to engage the outlaws anew.

The Merrymen took to the woods as Robin and Much the miller's son strove to get Littlejohn into the safety of the greenwood. The constables perceived that only three of the outlaws were still in the clear, and descended toward where Littlejohn lay wounded in the road.

"Robin, you must save yourself," Littlejohn pleaded. "I cannot move out of the way to save myself. So leave me here.

"But, before you leave, I pray, for God's sake, do not allow the proud sheriff's forces to take me alive. Take out your sword and drive it through my heart. If you ever loved me, and would reward me for my full-hearted service to you, grant me the gift of death with honor."

"That I will not do, John," Robin replied. "I will not slay you. Nor will the sheriff's men lay a hand on you. Here, Much. Help me get our wounded companion into the safety of the woods."

Robin and Much hauled Littlejohn into the relative safety of the greenwood. The sheriff's men could not pursue through the thicket on horseback, so followed on foot, loosing arrows after the fleeing outlaws.

Robin carried his stricken companion on his back, but had to set him down and have Much assist him from time to time. He shot arrows back at the pursuers at intervals, but was unable to dissuade them in their pursuit.

Not too far into the greenwood there was a double-moated, walled castle. And dwelling in that castle was Sir Richard of Lee. He was the very same knight Robin had lent the four hundred pounds to under the trystell-tree.

Sir Richard had spied Robin and his men being chased by the sheriff's men. He had the drawbridges lowered over the moats, opened the castle doors, and allowed all of Robin Hood's men into the safety of the castle. Robin and Much just barely got Littlejohn through the portcullis when the drawbridges were raised, leaving the law officers unable to get to any of the outlaws.

Sir Richard welcomed Robin and his men.

"There is no one in the world," he told Robin, "I love as I love you. I am eternally grateful for the help you gave me when I was in my most desperate state. You and your men shall remain safe in this castle despite the sheriff. The gates shall be shut, the bridges shall be drawn. And I will arm you and your men to withstand any assault.

Robin and the men were safe behind the walls. They were well taken care of for there was food, drink, beds, and shelter aplenty.

And Littlejohn's wound was attended to with care and skill.

When the constables returned to Nottingham town to tell the sheriff how they had come close to capturing Littlejohn, the proud lawman was not happy. When he was told that they had nearly even captured Robin Hood as he was carrying his wounded henchman on his back through the greenwood, the sheriff grew unhappier still. And when it was revealed that Robin, Littlejohn and a host of the Merrymen had been welcomed by Sir Richard of Lee into his castle and were being harbored there by the knight, the sheriff set out with a large contingent to demand that Sir Richard turn the outlaws over to him.

After the sheriff's men surrounded Castle Lee, the sheriff called out to Sir Richard:

"Sir Richard, within your walls you harbor the enemies of the king. By law and by right, I demand that you release them to my custody. Else you are a traitor to the realm and unworthy as a knight."

Sir Richard stood atop the battlement and addressed the sheriff in thundering voice:

"What I have done, Sir, I have done appropriate to my vows as a true knight. I do not accept your jurisdiction over me. I am a nobleman answerable only to our liege lord, King Richard of the Lion Heart. You are free to address your charge to His Majesty. But until I have orders from the king only, I will entertain whom I will within my lands and castle."

The sheriff had to acknowledge that under the law Sir Richard was subject only to the king. So he withdrew his men from Sir Richard's lands and rode off to London to address his grievance to Good King Richard, he of the Lion's Heart.

Although the sheriff's troops had withdrawn, Robin felt it would be unsafe to leave the castle until he was sure there was not a trap awaiting him out in the greenwood. And, at any rate, until Littlejohn's wounded knee was whole again, it would be wise to remain sequestered in the castle.

One fine morning, after breakfast, when Robin had returned to his quarters within the keep, Sir Richard came to visit him, bearing pleasant news.

"Robin," he chortled. "A guest has made herself present without the walls. We have admitted her."

Robin could not imagine what such news might portend for him.

"Is this new guest someone you would have me meet, Milord?" he asked.

"Hardly," the knight smiled. "It seems the maid knows you well already. Or so she claims."

"Is it perchance my true love?" Robin asked. "Could it be Maid Marian?"

That response brought a jolly laugh from the gentle knight's belly.

"Whether she be your true-love or not, my friend, I know not. What I do know is that the name she claims as her own is not Marian."

Robin wondered who, then, it could be. And asked his host that very question.

"The lass says her name is Rosalind and that back in Locksley she heard of your recent encounter with our sheriff and your subsequent tenancy in Castle Lee. She has come to inquire about your well-being."

Rosalind! It had been many a year since Robin had thought about Rosalind and his frolics with her in the hayloft. He requested Sir Richard to have her led to his private quarters in the keep.

"Gladly," Sir Richard agreed. And he departed the room in high good humor.

At a rap, Robin threw open the door. And there Rosalind was in all her buxom beauty.

Robin strove valiantly to remain true to his Maid Marian. There was a mighty struggle between his will and his lust.

The moment Rosalind removed her blouse and jiggled her titties at him, lust won. Hands down.

Robin remembered that a long time back he had gone to fetch a butt of good October ale to Rosalind, expecting a genuine basic fuck in return.

While it was true that circumstances had prevented him from returning with the ale, he still felt he deserved the promised fuck from her.

Here Rosalind was in Sir Richard's castle, and in Robin's room within the castle.

She had lain down completely disrobed, and her oozing cunt was beckoning at his inflamed dick.

For the next five days, Robin had reclaimed the deserved but formerly denied fuck of yesteryear manifold.

He allowed no one in his room as he claimed his just reward, again, and again, and again.

In due course, Much the miller's son came to Robin's door and beckoned him outside.

"Yes, Much," Robin replied in a surly tone. "I am quite occupied at the moment and do not wish to be disturbed."

"Everyone in the castle is aware of how absorbed you have been with matters-at-hand in recent days, Master," Much replied. "But I felt you needed to know that a new visitor has arrived at Lee Castle asking for you."

"Not the proud sheriff, I hope!" Robin exclaimed.

"No," Much answered. "She does not seem to be an envoy from the sheriff."

She?! Could it be? Surely not Maid Marian.

Robin would rather it be the sheriff himself than Maid Marian while he had Rosalind in his quarters.

But he was assured that it was, indeed, Marian who had come to Castle Lee.

Robin rushed back into his chambers.

"Quickly, Rosalind," he urged. "Word is that the sheriff is approaching the castle with a mighty force. It is not clear whether we can withstand the assault. It is unsafe for you to remain here. You must leave immediately. My cohort, Much, will lead you away to the safety of Locksley. Quick, quick! You dare not remain a second longer here. Your life and chastity are in danger if are not on your way home within minutes."

Rosalind was convinced and moved by Robin's exhortation. And she was forthwith spirited away from Castle Lee by Much. As she and Much hurried past the waiting Maid Marian, neither lass paid great attention to the other. They were too preoccupied with their own concerns.

Once Much and Rosalind were well out of the way, Will Scarlet brought Maid Marian to Robin's door.

Like Rosalind, Marian had been made aware of Robin's plight. Of how the sheriff and his men had driven her love into Castle Lee. She had arrived, aware of the danger, to give succor to her lover.

Marian never realized what danger was narrowly avoided by her arrival.

The truth was, Maid Marian was a far better fuck than Rosalind. And much more inventive of variations in lovemaking.

And what was more, the variation she had devised in her cottage back in Nottingham had evolved to be one that Robin now asked for frequently. And which she was delighted to agree to.

And for the length of Robin's stay at the castle, Marian gave him great comfort. Not only sexual, but emotional as well.

While Robin was beset with a potential romantic disaster should Rosalind return, the sheriff completed his voyage to London and to the throneroom of the king.

He told King Richard about Robin Hood and his lawless deeds. He went on to tell how the outlaws shot the king's deer with impunity.

"This outlaw is presently under the protection of Sir Richard of Lee," he went on to explain,. "Sir Richard has set himself above the law, Your Majesty. I fear that if there is not royal intervention, Sir Richard will set himself up as ruler of the north country. And that outlaws will drive the realm into anarchy."

Richard the Lion-Hearted listened well to the sheriff's plea and was moved to action.

"Good sheriff," he said. "I am convinced by your tale. I promise you that within two weeks' time I will come to Nottingham. And while I am there, I will take this Robin Hood and Sir Richard and make examples of them. Return now to Nottingham and await my arrival."

A very satisfied sheriff returned to his shire that day.

During the two week period that the sheriff awaited the king's arrival, Littlejohn's wound healed very nicely. Scouts determined that there were no constables lurking in the greenwood, and Robin felt sure it would be safe to return to his haunts in Sherwood.

He could not convince Maid Marian to join him yet in that sylvan realm. So she was escorted to her cottage in Nottingham town by Much and Will Scarlet.

Robin thanked his host for all his courtesy. And Castle Lee became again a quiet fortress.

Robyn Hode walked in the forest
Under the levys grene.
The proude sheryfe of Notyngham
Thereof he had grete tene.

The sheryfe there faled of Robyn Hode.
He myght nat have his pray.
Than he awaited this gentyll knyght
Bothe by nyght and day.

Ever he wayted the gentyll knyght,
Syr Richarde at the lee,
As he went on haukynge bi the ryvyr-syde
And lete his haukës flee.

Toke he there his gentyll knyght
With men of armys stronge,
And led hym to Notynghamwarde
Bound bothe fote and honde.

The sheryfe sware a full grete othe,

Bi hym that dyed on rode,
He had lever than a hundred pound
That he had Robyn Hode.

This harde the knyghtës wyfe,
A fayr lady and a fre.
She set hyr on a gode palfrey
To grene wode anone rode she.

Whanne she cam in the forest,
Under the grene wode tre,
Fonde she there Robyn Hode
And al his fayre menë.

"God the save, gode Robyn
And all thy compani.
For Oure dere Ladyes sake
A bone graunte thou me.

"Late never my wedded lorde
Shamefully slayne be.
He is fast bound to Nottynghamewarde
For the love of the."

Anone than sayde gode Robyn
To that lady fre,
"What man hath your lorde ytake?"
"The proude sheryfe," than sayd she.

. . . .

"For soth as I the say
He is nat yet thre mylës
Passed on his way."

Up than sterte gode Robyn
As man that had ben wode.
"Buske you, my mery men,
For hym that dyed on rode.

"And he that this sorrowe forsaketh,
By hym that dyed on tre,
Shal he never in grene wode

No lenger dwel with me."

Sone there were gode bowës bent,
Mo than seven score.
Hedge ne dyche spared they none
That was them before.

"I make myn avowe to God," sayde Robyn
"The sheryfe would I fayne se.
And if I may him take,
I-quyt than shall he be."

And whan they cam to Notyngham,
They walked in the street.
And with the proude sheryfe i-wys
Sonë can they mete.

"Abyde, thou proude sheryfe," he sayde.
"Abyde and speke with me.
Of some tydyngs of oure kinge
I wolde fayne here of the.

"This seven yere, by dere worthy God,
Ne yede I this fast on fote.
I make myn avowe to God, thou proude sheryfe,
It is not for thy gode."

Robyn bent a ful gode bowe,
An arrowe he drowe at wyll.
He hit so the proude sheryfe
Upon the grounde he lay full styll.

And or he might up aryse
On his fete to stoned,
He smote of the sheryfes hede
With his bright bronde.

"Lye thou there, thou proude sheryfe.
Evyll mote thou thryve.
There myght noo man to the truste
The whyles thou were alive."

Hys men drewe out theyr bright swerdes

That were so sharpe and kene,
And layde on the sheryves men
And dryved them down bydene.

Robyn stert to that knyght,
And cut a two his bonde,
And toke hym in his honde a bowe,
And bad hym by hym stoned.

"Leve thy hors the behynde,
And lerne for to renne.
Thou shalt with me to grene wode
Through myre, mosse, and fenne.

"Thou shalt with me to grene wode,
Without any leasynge,
Tyll that I have gete us grace
Of [Rycharde], our comly kynge.

A Gest of Robyn Hode
The Sixth Fytte

CHAPTER THIRTEEN

The Capture of Sir Richard

Robin was back in his forest home with all his Merrymen. The sheriff was an annoyance, but no immediate threat. There had been no sign that the sheriff was any more able to search him out now than he ever had been.

The sheriff, believing that the king's forces would soon eliminate his nemesis, turned his attention to an enemy he thought he *could* capture. Sir Richard of Lee.

So he sent spies familiar with the intricacies of the greenwood to watch Castle Lee. They were to observe without being observed.

One of his spies reported that Sir Richard was feeling safe from the sheriff's intrusion now that his castle no longer was a refuge for Robin's outlaws. He was leaving his castle on horseback daily to pursue his favorite sport, hawking.

Sir Richard grew comfortable riding along the river and loosing his hawks to retrieve prey.

The sheriff and a contingent of speedy horsemen lay in wait for the next jaunt of the knight in pursuit of his sport.

And on a certain day, the sheriff and his men descended swiftly on the sportsman just as he was sending his hawks into the sky.

They seized him, bound him hand and foot, and spirited him unceremoniously off to Nottingham town.

The sheriff was pleased by the capture of the nobleman who had lorded it over him. But he swore that the great prize had not yet been won. He would rather have Robin Hood in his clutches than the windfall of a hundred pounds.

Sir Richard's wife was apprized of her husband's capture by a groom who had managed to escape when the knight was taken. The dame immediately mounted her palfrey and headed for the greenwood. She knew the way to the Great Oak and rode directly there. When she arrived she found Robin and his entire band.

"God save you, Robin," she greeted. "And may all your company thrive. I have come to ask a boon of you, for Our Dear Lady's sake.

"My husband has been captured, bound fast, and hauled to Nottingham town. He was abducted because of his love for you. I have come to seek your aid to see that my wedded lord be not slain in shameful fashion."

Robin asked who was responsible for this outrage.

"It was, and is, the proud sheriff," the dame told him. "The arrest was very recent. The troops that took my lord and trussed him up may not be more than three miles up the highway even as we speak."

Robin assembled his men immediately and addressed them.

"To horse, good yeomen. I swear by God Almighty that if any man of you shrinks from the task of re-capturing Sir Richard, he shall never more be welcomed by me here in the greenwood."

His seven score men responded with bent bow and followed Robin straight through the forest, meeting no impediment on the way.

Robin swore a great oath aloud.

"I swear to God that I shall encounter the sheriff. And when I find him, I will exact my revenge on him."

When the troop arrived in Nottingham town, it rode directly up the High Street directly to the gaol. The Merrymen assembled in the square outside the prison where they encountered the sheriff and a full contingent of his men.

The skirmish between the Sherwood outlaws and the Nottingham lawmen was bitter and intense.

Robin and the sheriff met horse to horse, bow to bow, and sword to sword.

When the troops on both sides became aware that the two chiefs had met person-to-person, they withdrew as custom decrees to allow the two avowed enemies to settle their long-standing enmity.

"Here we are, at last, proud sheriff, face-to-face," Robin challenged. "For seven years now, fate has kept us at a distance from one another. Now, destiny has brought us together. And, God willing, proud sheriff, our meeting will end with your demise."

The two rivals dismounted and faced each other as the constables and the Merrymen observed in solemn silence.

The enemy chiefs each notched an arrow. Robin's shaft loosed first, while the sheriff's slight delay caused his arrow to miss Robin Hood.

Robin's arrow flew straight and true, wounding the sheriff just below his heart and felling him to the ground.

Robin drew his sword and strode up to his fallen enemy. As the wounded sheriff strove with what energy he had left to arise, Robin's sword sliced through the lawman's neck.

"Lie there, proud sheriff," Robin exclaimed. "And evil betake your soul. Whilst you were alive, that evil abided with you. Now, thanks be to God, I am avenged of you."

As Robin stepped away from the decapitated corpse, fighting resumed between Robin's men and the constables. In short order, the sheriff's men were defeated and Robin entered the gaol. There he found the knight still bound hand and foot.

Robin severed the bonds and helped Sir Richard to his feet.

"Come, Sir Richard," he said. "Let us to the safety of the greenwood. You shall be free there from any harm until I am able to plead your case in person before our comely king. He will see the justice of your case and restore you to full freedom again."

And with that assurance, Sir Richard of Lee and his dame accommodated themselves to the bucolic life of Sherwood Forest until such time as King Richard might set matters aright for them.

The kynge cam to Notyngham
With knygthes in grete araye,
For to take that gentyll knyght
And Robyn Hode, and yf he may.

He asked men of that countrë
After Robyn Hode.
And after that gentyll knight
That was go bolde and stout.

Whan they had tolde hym the case
Our kynge understode thyer tale,
And seased in his honde
The knythtës londës al.

All the passe of Lancassshyre
He went both ferre and nere,
Tyl he cam to Plompton Parke
He faylyd many of his dere.

There our kynge was sont to se
Herdës many one.
He coud unneth fynde one dere
That bare ony gode horne.

The kynge was wonder wroth with al
And swore by the Trynytë,
"I would I had Robyn Hode
With iyn I myght hym se.

"And he that wolde smyte of the knyghtës hede
And brynge it to me
He shall have the knythtës londes,
Syr Rycharde at the Le.

"I gyve it hym with my charter
And sele it with my honde,
To have and holde for ever mere
In all mery Englonde."

Than bespake a fayre olde knyght
That was trewe in his fay.
"A, my leegë lorde the kynge
One worde I shal you say.

"There is no man in this countrë
May have the knyghtës londes
Whyle Robyn Hode may ryde or gone
And bere a bowe in his hondes.

"That he ne shal lese his hede
That is the best ball in his hode,
Give it noo man, my lorde the kynge
That ye wyll any gode."

Half a yere dwelled our comly kynge
In Notyngham, and well mere,
Coude he not here of Robyn Hode
In what countrë he were.

Alway went good Robyn
By halke and eke by hyll,
And always slew the kyngës dere,
And welt them at his wyll.

Than bespake a proude fostere,
That stode by our kyngës kne,

"Yf ye wyll se gode Robyn,
"Ye must do after me.

"Take five of the best knyghtes
"That be in your lede,
"And walke downe by yon abbay,
"And gete you monkës wede.

"And I wyll be your ledes-man
"And lede you the way.
"And or ye come to Notyngham,
"Myn hede then dare I lay,

"That ye shall mete with gode Robyn,
"On lyve yf that he be,
"Or ye come to Notyngham,
"With iyn ye shal hym se."

Full hastely our kynge was dyght,
So were his knyghtës five,
Everych of them in monkës wede,
And hasted them thyder blyve.

Our kynge was grete above his cole,
A brode hat on his crowne,
Ryght as he were abbot-lyke,
They rode up into the towne.

Styf botes our kynge had on,
Forsoth as I you say.
He rode syngynge to grene wode,
The covent was clothed in graye.

His male-hors and his grete somers
Folowed our kynge behynde,
Tyll they came to grene wode,
A myle under the lynde.

There they met with gode Robyn,
Stondynge on the waye,
And so dyde many a bolde archere,
For soth as I you say.

Robyn toke the kyngës hors,
Hastely in that stede,
And sayde, "Syr abbot, by your leve,
"A whyle ye must abyde.

"We be yemen of this foreste,
"Under the grene-wode tre.
"We lyve by our kyngës dere,
"Other shift have not wee.

"And ye have chyrches and rentës both,
"And gold full grete plentë.
"Gyve us some of your spendynge,
"For seynt charytë."

Than bespake our cumly kynge,
Anone than sayde he,
"I brought noo mere to grene-wode
But forty pounde with me.

"I have layne at Notyngham,
"This fourtynyght with our kynge,
"And spent I have full moche gode
"On many a grete lordynge.

"And I have but forty pounde,
"Noo mere than have I me.
"But if I had an hundred pounde,
"I would give it to the."

Robyn toke the forty pounde,
And departed it in two partye,
Halfendell he gave his mery men,
And bad them mery to be.

Full curteysly Robyn gan say;
"Syr, have this for your spendyng;
"We shall mete another day."
"Gramercy," than sayde our kynge.

"But well the greteth Edward [Richard], our kynge,
"And sent to the his seale,
"And byddeth the com to Notyngham,

"Both to mete and mele."

He toke out the brode targe,
And sone he lete hym se.
Robyn coud his courteysy,
And set hym on his kne.

"I love no man in all the worlde
"So well as I do my kynge.
"Welcome is my lordës seale;
"And, monke, for thy tydynge,

"Syr abbot, for thy tydynges,
"To day thou shal dyne with me,
"For the love of my kynge,
"Under my trystell-tre."

Forth he lad our comly kynge,
Full fayre by the honde.
Many a dere there was slayne,
And full fast dyghtande.

Robyn toke a full grete horne,
And loude he gan blowe.
Seven score of wyght younge men
Cam redy on a rowe.

All they kneled on theyr kne,
Full fayre before Robyn.
The kynge sayd hym selfe untyll,
And swore by Seynt Austyn,

'Here is a wonder semely syght;
"Me thynketh, by Goddës pyne,
"His men are mere at his byddynge
"Then my men be at myn."

Full hastely was theyr dyner idyght,
And thereto gan they gone.
They served our kynge with al theyr myght,
Both Robyn and Lytell Johann.

Anone before our kynge was set

The fattë venison,
The gode white brede, the good rede wyne,
And therto the fyne ale and browne.

"Make good chere," said Robyn,
"Abbot, for charytë.
"And for this ylke tydynge,
"Blyssed mot thou be.

"Now shalt thou se what lyfe we lede,
"Or thou hens wende,
That thou may enforme our kynge,
"Whan ye togyder lende."

Up they sterte al in hast,
Theyr bowes were smartly bent.
Our kynge was never so sore agast,
He wende to have be shente.

Two yerdes there were up set,
Thereto gan they gange,
By fifty pase, our kynge sayde,
The merkës were to longe.

On every syde a rose-garlonde,
They shot under the lyne.
"Who so fayleth of the rose-garlonde," sayde Robyn,
"His takyll he shall tyne.

"And yelde it to his mayster,
"Be it never so fyne,
"For no man wyll I spare,
"So drynke I ale or wyne;

"And here a buffet on his hede,
"I-wys ryght all bare."
And all that fell in Robyns lote,
He smote them wonder sare.

Twyse Robyn shot aboute,
And ever he cleved the wande,
And so dyde good Gylberte
With the whytë honde.

Lytell Johann and gode Scathelocke, [Will Scarlet]
For nothynge wolde they spare.
Whan they fayled of the garlonde,
Robyn smote them full sore.

At the last shot that Robyn shot,
For all his frendës fare,
Yet he fayled of the garlonde
Thre fingers and a mare.

Than bespake good Gylberte,
And thus he gan say,
"Mayster," he sayde, "your takyll is lost,
"Stande forth and take your pay."

"Yf it be so," sayde Robyn,
"That may no better be,
"Syr abbot, I delyver the myn arowe,
"I pray the, syr, serve thou me."

"It falleth not for myn ordre," sayde our kynge,
"Robyn, by thy leve,
"For to smyte noo gode yeman,
"For doute I should hym greve."

"Smyte on boldely," sayde Robyn,
"I give the large leve."
Anone our kynge, with that worde,
He folde up his sleve,

And sych a buffet he gave Robyn,
To grounde he yede full nere.
"I make myn avowe to God," sayde Robyn,
"Thou are a stalworthe frere.

"There is pith in thyn arme," sayde Robyn,
"I trowe thou canst well shete."
Thus our kygne and Robyn Hode
Togeder gan they mete.

Robyn behelde our comly kynge
Wystly in the face,

And so dyde Syr Rycharde at the Le
And kneled down in that place.

And so dyde all the wylde outlawes
Whan they se them knele.
"My lorde the kynge of Englonde
Now I knowe you wel."

"Mercy then, Robyn," sayde our kynge
"Under your trystell-tre,
Of thy goodnesse and thy grace
For my men and me!"

"Yes, for God," sayde Robyn,
"And also God me save.
I aske mercy my lorde the kynge
For my men I crave."

"Yes, for God, than sayde our kynge,
"And therto sent I me
With that thou leve the grene-wode
And all thy company.

"And come home, syr, to my courte,
And there dwell with me."
"I make myn avowe to God," sayd Robyn,
"And ryght so shall it be.

"I wyll com to your courte,
Your servyse for to se,
And brynge with me of my men
Seven score and thre.
"But me lyke well your servyse
I wyll come agayne full soone
And shote at the donnë dere
As I am wonte to done."

A Geste of Robyn Hode
The Seventh Fytte
Circa 1300 A.D.

CHAPTER FOURTEEN

The King Comes to Nottingham

As he had promised the now defunct sheriff, King Richard I came to Nottingham accompanied by a huge contingent of knights. He had come with the express purpose of capturing Sir Richard of Lee and Robin Hood and putting an end to their rebellious behavior.

After making local inquiries, he seized all of Sir Richard's lands and held them as royal possessions that might be passed on to a less troublesome subject.

He progressed through the north country to see how his hunting grounds fared. He went through Lancaster and up to Plumton Park. In all his forest lands he spotted nary a mature deer.

The king was wroth to discover the extent of the poaching of his herds and swore by the Trinity:

"I will see this Robin Hood with my own eyes. And as to Sir Richard of Lee, I would have his head. Whoever brings me that caitiff lord's head shall be awarded his land. I will give it to him with my charter and seal it with my hand to have and to hold forevermore in merry England."

An elderly knight who was unafraid to speak his mind said to his sovereign:

"My liege lord. I would have a word with you. For as long as Robin Hood rides in the surroundings with bow in hand, anyone who usurps Sir Richard's domain will soon find his head severed from his body. If you wish to grant a favor to any subject as a reward, do *not* grant him title to Castle Lee and its surroundings."

King Richard remained a half year in Nottingham but was unable to get any information concerning Robin Hood's whereabouts.

But Robin was unfazed by the king's concerns. He rode through the king's forest at will. He had his hiding places. But he hardly remained hidden out of sight most of the time. And he shot the king's deer with impunity.

One of the king's foresters came to the monarch when he was in Mansfield. He explained that there was one sure way to encounter Robin Hood.

"My liege lord," he said. "If you would really like to see Robin Hood, I can tell you exactly how to go about it.

"Take five knights from your company and go with them to the abbey down the way. There, don monks' robes. All six of you. And you, Sire, should bear a purse beneath your robes. And in that purse carry forty pounds.

"Once disguised as monks, I will lead you down the highway towards Nottingham. And before we arrive at Nottingham, I assure you we shall meet Master Robin."

Richard's lion heart rejoiced at the prospect of such an adventure. So, with five of his most trusted knights, he went to the abbey. The small troop donned monks' weeds and the monarch carried the forty pounds in his wallet.

Led by the wise forester, the curious troop rode along the highway on their mounts, laughing and jesting about the jolly adventure. With the gay talk, the laughter, and the dust of the road, King Richard developed a great thirst.

"By the Rood," he said in a loud voice. "I am as thirsty as a dry reed. I would gladly give forty pounds for something to quench my thirst."

The words were scarcely out of his mouth when a reddish-blond tall fellow stepped out of the forest onto the highway and took hold of the king's bridle rein.

"Welcome, holy brother," said the intruder. "It seems your prayer is answered. We keep a novel inn within the forest. For forty pounds we can offer you red wine, fine brown ale, and wonderfully roasted venison."

Robin[9], for it was he who had accosted the king, put two fingers to his mouth and let loose a high, shrill whistle.

Out of the greenwood sprang a score of green-clad archers, surrounding the king and his party.

"You see, reverend brother," quoth Robin, "we are jocund yeomen who live by the grace of our good king's deer. I would relieve you of the forty pounds you mentioned. And, for your part, you may consider it charity."

King Richard answered that forty pounds was all he had on him.

"I have recently been with the king in Nottingham Town," the king explained, "and I have spent a great deal of money there while in his company. These forty pounds are all I have left."

9   The meeting between Robin Hood of Locksley Hall and King Richard I, the Lion Hearted, occurred on the Lincoln Highway, Nottinghamshire, on May 5, 1190.

Robin was impressed, because even though an outlaw, he respected the rulers of his land.

"Sir Abbot," he said. "I honor our king above all men on this earth. In honor of him, you and your fellow brothers shall dine with me this day at a cut rate. Hand me your purse."

The king reached beneath his robe, pulled out the purse, and handed it to Robin.

Robin opened it and removed twenty pounds.

"I will keep twenty pounds as your charity contribution to the welfare of me and my men, and for those poor folk who depend on us. But the remaining twenty pounds I return to you lest we leave you destitute."

Robin handed the half-filled purse back to King Richard and blew on his horn. Littlejohn and a score more of Robin's men sprang out of the forest and bent their knee to their chief.

"By Saint Augustine," Richard muttered. "This man's entourage is a better disciplined group than any of my own regiments."

Robin and the Merrymen led the disguised king and his knights into Sherwood Forest to the Great Oak. There Pym was roasting venison and his helpers were setting out tuns of ale and wine. For, at the time, Robin had laid in a store of wine for the pleasure of the guests he ushered in from the highways and lanes, after relieving them of their wealth.

When Robin and his retinue arrived at the Trystell-tree with their new guests, Pym was preparing a feast and the Merrymen who had remained in the greenwood were anticipating a savory meal.

Gilbert of the White Hand had accepted Robin's invitation to visit the haunts of Sherwood Forest and happened to be present at the tables when the king appeared. King Richard was astonished to see him there among the outlaws, but, of course, said nothing to indicate his surprise. Gilbert did not recognize his king, disguised in Blackfriar habit.

The prepared feast was served to the entire host, with Robin and King Richard at the head table. The five knights in Blackfriar robes sat to their right and left.

Robin proposed a toast.

"Long live our noble king, Richard of the Lion-Heart."

The throng raised their horns and enthusiastically shouted the toast back, followed by exclamations of "hear, hear."

King Richard was gratified by the loyalty of these rough men of the forest.

"As a guest at the head table," Richard asked, "May I request that one of your men join me at my left hand that I may learn from him about the life your men lead in the greenwood?"

"Of course, Holy Abbot," Robin replied. "Would you care to choose one of my men? We would have you take word back to our king about the ways of our brotherhood. Choose at your will."

The king pointed out David of Doncaster, who was told to come to the head table and entertain the head guest. David presented himself and room was made for him to the left of the guest of honor.

The feast was served and King Richard felt he had seldom eaten or drunk so well, or in better company.

David of Doncaster was pleased to inform Richard about the pleasures of the free life the band lived in the greenwood. King Richard nearly envied the life led by these rough Saxon subjects of his.

When the meal was over, Robin was intent, as always, to entertain his guests.

"Sir Abbot," he said. "For after-dinner entertainment, we propose an archery contest, that you may report to our newly crowned king that he has subjects in Sherwood Forest who can shoot straight and true. We demonstrated our skill to his majesty's royal parents at Finsbury Field some time ago. Would you enjoy such an exhibition here?"

King Richard was an excellent bowman himself, and expressed great interest in seeing the Merrymen exhibit their archery skill.

"David," Robin said to the king's table companion. "Prepare a rose garland and post it on yonder oak some fifty paces distant. It shall be our target."

David left the table and set up the floral target.

"Let's see now," Robin mused. "Who will we choose to demonstrate our sharpshooting skills? Our guest Gilbert, while a temporary guest with us, shall lead off to demonstrate that the king's men know a straight from a crooked arrow. Following him, let Littlejohn shoot. His style should amuse our guests and astound them with his accuracy. Will Scarlet shall follow Littlejohn. Then I will conclude the exhibition with mine own bow. He who misses the center of the garland shall receive such a buffet from me that he will remember to shoot truer hereafter."

Gilbert of the White Hand toed the mark first. He unleashed three arrows that hit the very center of the floral target.

"Well done," said Robin. "I wish you would become one of our band. But I respect your choice to serve our sovereign lord, King Richard, in his regiment. It is said you and he will leave soon on Crusade to rid the Holy Land of the Infidel. Our liege lord can use such true marksmanship in his army."

The entire band applauded. As did the king and his knights.

Next Littlejohn stepped up to the mark. He had been drinking lustily throughout the feast. He unloosed three arrows in rapid succession and all three totally missed the mark.

Robin smote Littlejohn on the head with such force it knocked the huge man flat onto the ground. The mob roared with laughter.

Next it was Will Scarlet's turn. He had matched Littlejohn's imbibing horn for horn. He was unsteady on his feet at the mark. He shot his three missiles. Alas! All missed. The thwack Robin gave Will caused him to topple to uproarious laughter from the crowd.

"Now," Robin boasted. "I will demonstrate how temperance pays."

He toed the mark and shot two arrows into the target's center. But the third arrow was off by more than three fingers.

Gilbert of the White Hand spoke up.

"Good Master Robin," he said. "Your last arrow missed the mark. As declared by your own rules, you must pay."

"Quite right, Fair Gilbert," Robin agreed. "It is up to me to choose who shall pay me for my folly. And I elect our guest of honor."

King Richard protested.

"It would be against the rules of my order to do harm to a yeoman," the king declared.

"In this case, Sir Abbot, the yeoman gives you leave to smite him with your might. Your vows should not interfere when you have been requested to deliver the gift."

King Richard could not resist the opportunity. He rolled up his sleeve, revealing a much more muscled arm than Robin had counted on.

Robin closed his eyes in anticipation of the blow. And Richard gave a lion-hearted buffet that knocked Robin silly to the ground.

From the earthen floor Robin looked up at the personage who had delivered such a wallop.

"I vow, Sir Abbot," Robin laughed. "You must be the most stalwart friar in Christendom."

On arising from his fallen position, Robin examined the king's face thoughtfully. At the same time, Sir Richard of Lee also scrutinized the face. Both came to the same realization and knelt before their sovereign.

When the Merrymen saw what was happening, they all knelt down as well.

"My lord," quoth Robin. "I well know now who you are. You are the King of England."

The king replied, "And I stand here under your trystell-tree to thank you, Robin, for the kindness and courtesy you have shown to my men and to me."

"I ask then for clemency, my sovereign, for me and for my men."

"Yes, Robin," King Richard replied. "That I grant, providing you and your entire company leave the greenwood and come with me to court and dwell there with me."

"I swear by God," Robin replied, "that we will so do. I will accompany you along your return to London town with my seven score and three men, to

165

serve you at your pleasure.

"But if I find that service at the court turns out to be displeasing to me, I will return here to the greenwood and again shoot the deer as I have been doing."

"Haste thou ony grene cloth," sayd our kynge,
"That thou wylte sell nowe to me?"
"Ye, for God," sayde Robyn,
"Thyrty yerdes and thre."

"Robyn," sayde oure kynge,
"Now pray I the,
Sell me some of that cloth
To me and my meynë.

"Yes, for God," than sayde Robyn,
"Or elles I were a fole.
Another day ye wyll me clothe,
I trowe, ayenst the Yole."

The kynge kest of his cole than.
A grene garment he dyde on.
And every knyght also, iwys
Another had full sone.

Whan they were clothed in Lyncolne grene
They kest away theyr graye.
"Now we shal to Notyngham."
All thus our kynge gan say.

They bente theyr bowes and forth they went,
Shotynge all in-fere,
Towarde the towne of Notyngham,
Outlawes as they were.

Our kynge and Robyn rode togyder,
For soth as I you say.
And they shote pluke-buffet
As they went by the way.

And many a buffet our kynge wan
Of Robyn Hode that day.

And nothynge spared good Robyn
Our kynge when he did pay.

"So God me helpë," sayde oure kynge,
"Thy game is nought to lere.
I sholde not get a shote of the
Though I shote all this yere."

All the people of Notyngham
They stode and behelde.
They sawe nothynge but mantels of grene
That covered all the felde.

Than every man to other gan say,
"I drede our kygne be slone.
Come Robyn Hode to the towne, i-wys
On lyve he lefte never one."

Full hastely they began to fle,
Both yemen and knaves,
And olde wyves that might evyll goo,
They hypped on theyr staves.

The kynge loughe full fast,
And commaunded theym agayne.
Whan they se our comly kynge
I-wys they were full fayne.

They ete and dranke, and made them glad,
And sange with notes hye.
Than bespake our comly kynge
To Syr Richarde at the Lee.

He gave hym there his londe agayne,
A gode man he bad hym be.
Robyn thanked our comly kynge,
And set hym on his kne.

Had Robyn dwelled in the kynges courte
But twelve monethes and thre,
That he had spent an hundred pounde
And all his mennes fe.

In every place where Robyn came
Ever mere he layde downe,
Both for knyghtës and for squyers
To gete hym grete renowne.

By than the yere was al agone
He had no man but twayne.
Lytell Johann and good Scathelocke
With hym al for to gone.

Robyn sawe yonge men shote
Full faire upon a day.
"Alas!" than sayde gode Robyn,
"My welthe is went away.

"Somtyme I was an archere gode,
A styffe and eke a stronge.
I was compted the best archere
That was in mery Englonde.

"Alas!" than sayde gode Robyn.
"Alas and well a woo!
Yf I dwele lenger with the kynge
Sorowe wyll me sloo."

Forth than went Robyn Hode
Tyll he came to our kynge.
"My lorde the kynge of Englonde
Graunte me my askynge.

"I made a chapel in Bernysdale
That seemly is to se.
It is of Mari Magdaleyne,
And thereto wolde I be.

"I might never in this seven nyght
No tyme to slepe ne wynke.
Nother all these seven dayes
Nother ete ne drynke.

"Me longeth sore to Bernysdale,
I may not be therefro.
Barefote and wolwarde I have hyght

Thyder for to go."

"Yf it be so," than sayde oure kynge,
"It may no better be.
Seven nyght I gyve the leve
No lengre, to dwell fro me."

Gramercy, lorde, than sayde Robyn,
And set hym on his kne.
He toke his leve full courteysly
To grene wode than went he.

Whan he came to grene wode
In a mery mornynge,
There he herde the notes small
Of byrdës mery syngynge.

'It is ferre gone," sayde Robyn,
"That I was last here.
Me lyste a lytell for to shote
At the donnë dere."

Robyn slewe a full grete harte.
Hys horne than gan he blow,
That all the outlawes of that forest
That horne coud they knowe,

And gadred them togyder
In a lytell throwe.
Seven score of wyght yonge men
Cam redy on a rowe.

And fayre dyde of they theyr hodes,
And set them on theyr kne.
"Welcome," they sayde, "our mayster,
Under this grene-wode tre."

. . . .

Cryst have mercy on his soule
That dyed on the rode!
For he was a gode outlawe
And dyde pore men moch gode.

169

A Geste of Robyn Hode
The Eighth Fytte
Circa 1300 A.D.

CHAPTER FIFTEEN

Off to London

The king asked Robin, "Do you have any green cloth that you will sell me?"

"Yes, Sire," Robin answered. "I have thirty three yards worth."

"Then, Robin," the king asked. "Sell me some of that cloth for me and my men to wear."

"I would be a fool to say no to that, by God," Robin exclaimed. "The time is coming when you are going to give me clothes for Christmas when I am at court."

The king was forthwith dressed in green as were his five knights. When they were all dressed in Lincoln green they discarded their gray monk's robes.

"Now, then," King Richard announced. "We are all off to Nottingham together."

Then, appearing to be a gang of outlaws, they rode up the highway towards Nottingham, shooting arrows along the way. The king and Robin rode side by side shooting a game of pluck-bucket as they went. The forfeit of the pluck for missing a target got exchanged nearly evenly between the king and the outlaw. The king, however, had to admit that Robin still managed to out-shoot him.

As the group rode into Nottingham, the people of the town saw that everyone riding in was garbed in green.

"I fear that our king has been slain," people began to say. "Robin Hood and his men are arriving here and have left the king and his companions slain in the greenwood."

The people in the streets all began to scatter, yeomen and churls, the fit and the lame.

The king was mightily amused and laughed aloud. Then he addressed the fleeing crowd. He commanded them to halt.

And when they observed him, the people rejoiced that their sovereign had returned unscathed.

They feasted, drank, and sang in gratitude.

Once back at his quarters, King Richard restored the lands he had confiscated back to Sir Richard of Lee. Robin was most thankful to his king and bent his knee in gratitude.

When Robin got to London with the king, his stay lasted fifteen months. In that time he managed to squander well over a hundred pounds. Every place he went, he spent lavishly and enjoyed the praise he got from the knights and squires of the city.

In that time, not only had he over-spent, but he had lost all his men back to the greenwood. Only Littlejohn and Will Scarlet remained with him.

Robin became despondent. He felt he was losing his strength and his shooting ability, both qualities wasted in city living. He even contemplated suicide.

Robin finally pulled himself together and went to the king.

"My lord and king," he pleaded. "I ask a boon of you. I had a chapel built in Barnsdale dedicated to Saint Mary Magdalene. I feel a great spiritual need to re-visit the chapel.

"For the past week I have been unable to sleep, eat, or drink. I must go to Barnsdale. I have been serving severe penance here in London for my past sins. I wear sack cloth and I go barefoot. I must visit my chapel in the north country."

The king was moved by Robin's plea.

"If such be the case, Robin," he said. "I grant you leave to go do what you feel you must do. But you must return to court within seven days."

Robin knelt before Richard, thanked him profoundly, and took his leave courteously.

Littlejohn and Will Scarlet had already left London, and Robin speedily rode down the highways, roads, and lanes that led from London to the greenwood he knew and loved. He trailed his two companions by several days.

When Robin arrived in Sherwood Forest, his greatest urge was to immediately shoot one of the king's dun deer.

He slew a hart, put his horn to his mouth, and blew the call that the Merrymen all recognized.

From out the forest, one at a time, his men assembled before him. The group was seven score strong.

They threw back their hoods and bowed the knee before their master.

"Welcome, Master," they shouted in unison. "Welcome back to your

rightful place under this greenwood tree."
      Robin Hood was back home again.

Sherwood in the twilight, is Robin Hood awake?
Grey and ghostly shadows are gliding through the brake,
Shadows of the dappled deer, dreaming of the morn,
Dreaming of a shadowy man that winds a shadowy horn.

Robin Hood is here again: all his merry thieves
Hear a ghostly bugle-note shivering through the leaves,
Calling as he used to call, faint and far away,
In Sherwood, in Sherwood, about the break of day.

Merry, merry England has kissed the lips of June:
All the winds of fairyland were here beneath the moon,
Like a flight of rose-leaves fluttering in a mist
Of opal and ruby and pearl and amethyst.

Merry, merry England is waking as of old,
With eyes of blither hazel and hair of brighter gold:
For Robin Hood is here again beneath the bursting spray
In Sherwood, in Sherwood, about the break of day.

Love is in the greenwood building him a house
Of wild rose and hawthorn and honeysuckle boughs:
Love is in the greenwood, dawn is in the skies,
And Marian is waiting with a glory in her eyes.

Hark! The dazzled laverock climbs the golden steep!
Marian is waiting: is Robin Hood asleep?
Round the fairy grass-rings frolic elf and fay,
In Sherwood, in Sherwood, about the break of day.

Oberon, Oberon, rake away the gold,
Rake away the red leaves, roll away the mould,
Rake away the gold leaves, roll away the red,
And wake Will Scarlett from his leafy forest bed.

Friar Tuck and Little John are riding down together
With quarter-staff and drinking-can and grey goose-feather.
The dead are coming back again, the years are rolled away
In Sherwood, in Sherwood, about the break of day.

Softly over Sherwood the south wind blows.
All the heart of England hid in every rose
Hears across the greenwood the sunny whisper keep,
Sherwood in the red dawn, is Robin Hood asleep?

Hark, the voice of England wakes him as of old
And, shattering the silence with a cry of brighter gold
Bugles in the greenwood echo in the steep,
Sherwood in the red dawn, is Robin Hood asleep?

Where the deer are gliding down the shadowy glen
All across the glades of fern he calls his merry men –
Doublets of the Lincoln green glancing through the May
In Sherwood, in Sherwood, about the break of day –

Calls them and they answer: from aisles of oak and ash
Rings the Follow! Follow! *and the boughs begin to crash,*
The ferns begin to flutter and the flowers begin to fly,
And through the crimson dawning the robber band goes by.

Robin! Robin! Robin! *All his merry thieves*
Answer as the bugle-note shivers through the leaves,
Calling as he used to call, faint and far away,
In Sherwood, In Sherwood, about the break of day

A Song of Sherwood
Alfred Noyes
1913 A.D.

CHAPTER SIXTEEN

Whither Robin?

The minstrels, balladeers, and storytellers who spread word of Robin Hood and his Merrymen are generally in accord with the tale up to the point of Robin leaving London and the king's court to return to Sherwood and Barnsdale. There are, however, several different conclusions to the tale after his return to the greenwood.

Some ballads record that Robin returned again to London and followed the king to the Holy Land. There is no ballad that mentions his return to England.

Still other songs are sung that tell that Robin married Maid Marian and that the two of them dwelt many years at Locksley Hall. These tales further tell that when Robin approached old age the Prioress of Kirklees foully murdered him with a poisoned draught.

But more tales than not end advising the listener that Robin Hood never died. That he continues to dwell in Sherwood Forest. It is said that on Saint Willibald's Eve, when there is a full moon illuminating the greenwood, Robin and his merry band gather together to feast and drink while Allan a Dale sings songs of the adventures they shared.

I, myself, do not know which of those endings is true. However, many years ago, I was enjoying a refreshing drink in a tavern in Mansfield. A minstrel entered the tavern and began to sing a tale of Robin that I had not run across before. When the minstrel had finished, I invited him to a pint or two of ale and asked him if he knew for sure what happened to Robin after he returned from London to Sherwood Forest.

"Indeed I do," the minstrel answered me. "For I saw Robin and his men with my very own eyes last Willibald Eve."

"Under the Great Oak, under the full moon?" I asked.

"That is where he and his Merrymen are to be found," I was assured.

I looked a bit skeptical.

"There are few who believe, and fewer still who have seen," the minstrel told me. "But go there yourself, and you will see fair Robin, Littlejohn, Will Stutely, Will Scarlet, Friar Tuck…all of them. They still feast and drink and revel in the music of Allan a Dale, the foremost minstrel who ever trod the lanes of our fair land."

I have not gone crawling through the forest, full moon or not, on any blessed saint's day. So, I cannot verify the man's story. Yet, Sherwood Forest still exists, and the Great Oak, the famed Trystell-tree stands to this day at its center. You can go, and see and hear for yourself.

O, I see the crescent promise of my spirit hath not set.
Ancient founts of inspiration well thro' all my fancy yet.
Howsoever these things be, a long farewell to Locksley Hall!
Now for me the woods may wither, now for me the roof-tree fall.
Comes a vapour from the margin, blackening over heath and holt,
Cramming all the blast before it, in its breast a thunderbolt.

Let it fall on Locksley Hall, with rain or hail, or fire or snow:
For the mighty wind arises, roaring seaward, and I go.

Locksley Hall
Alfred, Lord Tennyson

MIDDLE ENGLISH LEXICON

Middle English was the spoken and written language of England from around 1100 to about 1500. The earliest recorded ballads about Robin Hood were put to parchment in Middle English.

Words that did not survive in recognizable form into Elizabethan or later English are translated below.

almus – alms

Austyn – Augustine

avowë – patron

ayre – heir

behote – request

bested – unfavorably seen

betyme – soon/now

bode – invited

borowe – security/guarantee

broche – tapped and open

broke – enjoy

bryre – branch

buske – prepare

busshement – ambuscade

bydene – quickly

chorl – churl

coresed – caparisoned

corser – courser/horse

cun – grateful

curteyes – courtesy

derne strete – secret way

disgrate – fallen in fortune

dout – fear

dydly – deadly

dyght – prepare

dyghtande – prepared

eftsones – later/again

elle – ell (45 inches)

ellys – else

faylyd – missed

fayne – pleased

feders – feathers

fend – defend

(in) fere – together

ferre – far/stranger/foreigner

fone – foes

for – because

frees – prepare

fynly – goodly

gree – satisfaction

grome – man/groom

halke – hiding place

hede – head/safety

hendë – gentle/gracious

herken – harken

husbonde – farmer/ploughman/husband

hyght – promised

idyght – got ready

in-fere – together

inocked – notched

inowe – enough

int – in it

ipyght – offered as a prize

i-quyt – requited

iust – joust

i-wys – certainly

iyn – eyes

late – let

launsgay – lance

lede – company

lende – dwell

lere – cheeks/learn

lese – lose

lesynge – falsehood

let – delay

lever – rather

lorne – lost

lynde – linden

lythe – attend

lyve – alive

male – baggage

male-hors – pack horse

maugre – in spite of

medes – rewards

messis – masses

met – measured

meyne – men/company

molde – ground

moneth – month

mote – meeting

myrthës – entertainment/minstrelsy

myster – need

ne – nor

noo force – no matter

noumbles – entrails

okerer – usurer

ouris – hours

passé – extent

pay – satisfaction/liking

pluke-buffet – an archery game

prees – danger

prese – throng

pryckynge – lined up

pyne – passion

rawe – row

rede – red

renne – run

reve – despoil

reves – officials

rewë – rue

rewith – regret

sad – steadfast

seche – seek

seker – firm

set – shot

sette to wedde – pledged as security

shawe – copse

shend – punish

shente – injured

shope shaped

shrewed – cursed/damned

slist – slit

slone – slain

somers – pack horses

soriar – sorrier

staves – crutches

stede – place

stert – turn quickly

stertë – jumped/leaped

styrop – stirrups

syth – search

takles – arrows

targe – charter

tene – sorrow/annoyance

teris – tears

thryfte – luck

thyder blyve – quickly

tyne – lose

unkuth – unknown

unneth – hardly

wedes – clothes

wedde – pledge/bet

wende – go/thought

welt – controlled

wete – know

wode – mad/crazed

wolwarde – wearing wool next to the skin in pennance

wonnest – dwelleth

wyght – brave

wynne – go

wystly – thoughtfully

wyte – find out

ydyght – fitted

yeft – gift

Yole – Yule/Christmas

ylkë – same/very

About the Author

Tim Desmondes

Tim Desmondes is a Californian by birth and choice. He lives with his wife in a Southern California beach town.

He is a great believer in keeping his nose out of other people's business.

He welcomes the gradual diminution of puritanism (small p) and is less than cheerfully disposed towards prudery.

(What a philosopher!)

Nazca Plains Corporation has published five of his novels. *Inside Robin's Too Tight Tights* is the sixth.

- Sex and Loathing in Hollywood
- Sexual Diversity and Perversity in California
- Dracula Sucks Hollywood Dudes
- Venus Does Adonis While Apollo Shags a Tree
- Arthur Does Camelot

If you have not read all five of Tim's previously published books, what are you waiting for?